The Wedding Box

TONI BLAKE

Cover design: Dar Albert

All rights reserved.

Published by Oliver-Heber Books

0 9 8 7 6 5 4 3 2 1

To Jacquie, Marcie, and Renee,
for all the encouragement and support

Dear Reader,

After Covid and the deaths of both my parents, I didn't write for a while. Yes, I was busy clearing forty years of stuff from my girlhood home, but beyond that, the world just felt heavy to me and I had to take time to grieve. When I finally sat down to dip my toe back in the writing pool, I knew I needed to write something light and heartwarming, something that would lift me up and hopefully lift others up, too. What came out of me is The Wedding Box.

It's a much different sort of story than the angst-filled, heavy, and sometimes dark romances I'm known for writing. And it was only when I'd finished that I began to wonder: Will my readers like this? When they're used to one type of book from me, will they be open to another? And so I held on to this book for a while longer, turning that over in my head, and eventually seeking the advice of some trusted colleagues.

Not only did those colleagues tell me I *should* publish this book, but the current state of the world has me feeling like maybe it's the *perfect* time for something light and uplifting, that maybe we *all* need a feel-good story right now as much as *I* did when I wrote it.

And so my fondest wish is that The Wedding Box brings you joy and warmth, helps you escape from anything weighing you down at the moment, and leaves you believing in the good in life!

Sincerely,

Toni Blake

1
The Wedding

Haley

Aunt Nan has always said that sometimes we don't know what we want until it finds us.

Such a notion was utterly useless to me as a child—of course I knew what I wanted: chocolate ice cream, a kitten, snow days. Life was simpler then.

The idea took on a little more meaning years later when I was shopping for a lavender prom dress—it had to be lavender, in my vision it was lavender—but when my mother insisted I try on what I deemed an absolutely hideous red gown, to my surprise it looked fabulous, and I was the toast of Beechwood High for a night.

And what I unknowingly wanted found me in a much bigger way when it came to my career. I was certain I'd been born to be a fashionista—but turns out that loving clothes does not automatically translate into a job. I also imagined myself a high-powered businesswoman in some corporate setting in downtown Cincinnati, just a ten-minute drive from the suburb of Lakeside Park where I grew up. But only because that's what guidance counselors tell you to do if you have no particular passion: study business. Only when a nearby neighborhood bakery went on the market and my sister, Hannah, suggested we run it together did I realize *that* was my perfect career. I'm not even sure how I missed it. It made all the sense in the world. We both love to bake. We both have degrees in business. (Okay, thank you, guidance counselor.) We grew up baking with our mother and Aunt Nan, her older sister. We even took cake-decorating classes as teenagers—while other girls were kicking soccer balls up grassy fields or trying out for cheerleader, Hannah and I were busy sculpting the perfect buttercream rose. Spending my life behind the counter of the Two Sisters Bakery was clearly meant to be.

But when what I wanted *really, really* had to work to find me was when Ben entered my life. He's everything I never knew I was looking for. Which Aunt Nan has pointed out to me on a regular basis ever since our first date. Because *she* knew. She's like that.

And now, here I am, holding his hands in mine on a beautiful blue-sky summer day in front of all the people we both love. We're getting married!

"Welcome, friends. We're here today to witness the sacred union of Ben and Haley."

The wedding is taking place in my parents' backyard—which I *always* knew I wanted—and we stand before Pastor Tom beneath an arbor dripping with Blue Moon Kentucky wisteria. Beyond the arbor, where blossoms ripple in the lightest of June breezes, lies a tranquil pond where I ice-skated and swam as a girl.

Pastor Tom, a good-natured thirty-something guy who lives next door, continues with idyllic words about celebrating our love. Hannah is next to me, ravishing in pale lilac, while Ben's best friend and colleague, Terrence, stands at his side. Hannah's children, Cora and Cole, six and four, complete our little wedding party as flower girl and ring bearer. I look into Ben's eyes, feeling everything a bride should: happy, safe, ready, and bathed in love.

When Pastor Tom asks us to talk about our feelings for each other, my heart beats faster. I knew this was coming, but I don't often speak in front of crowds. Ben squeezes my hands reassuringly, reminding me with his gaze that it's all good.

"You are," I begin, our eyes still locked, "nothing like me at all." Everyone in the rows of white chairs before us chuckles gently as I explain. "And that's what makes you the perfect guy for me. You balance me out. When I'm impulsive, you're the man with the plan. When I'm clumsy, you steady me. When I'm sad, or afraid, you hold me up. You've become the rock I lean on, the person who makes me feel safe. You laugh at my jokes. You support my dreams. You think I'm *way* cooler than I am." More light laughter, which bolsters me for the rest. "I look forward to waking up each morning because I know you'll be part of my day. And even as different as we are in some ways, we want all the same things from life. I can't wait to start this next chapter with you."

When I'm done, his eyes smile into mine, and it hits me all over again that I get to keep him.

"Haley," Ben says, "when we met last year, I wasn't looking for a life partner. I'd lost a lot—my parents, my grandfather—and I truly thought I was meant to be a loner. And I was okay with that. I love my work, and I had a good enough life—better than I ever expected growing up. But you've given me...everything. Your laughter and silliness make me a more lighthearted guy. Your love and kindness give me a softer heart. Your sense of adventure keeps me from being a bore." As the crowd chuckles softly at that, he glances toward my parents in the front row. "Your family has become *my* family, just when I thought I'd never be a part of a family again."

My chest aches at his words. A private guy when it comes to personal stuff, Ben grumbled a little at the write-our-own-vows request from Pastor Tom, and I expected him to say something nice, but never so...open and *real.* I *do* give him a softer heart. And he *is* part of my family now. I already knew all that, but hearing it, and knowing *he* knows it, just makes my heart sing.

"I'm so grateful," he goes on, "to get to spend the rest of my life with you."

Pastor Tom says more pretty words, and we exchange rings, Ben's face framed by blue sky and purple wisteria as we say our 'I do's.

When Pastor Tom introduces us to the crowd a moment later as Mr. and Mrs. Benjamin Page, I take a moment to scan the crowd for my closest loved ones: my mom and dad, and of course Aunt Nan, who's worn an extravagant periwinkle hat today and looks happily weepy. I spot my bestie, Sienna—not in the wedding because she's a professional photographer and didn't trust anyone else to capture our day—crouched at the end of the petal-strewn grass aisle, snapping away behind her Nikon as Ben and I start toward her, hand in hand, husband and wife. I say a silent prayer: *May our existence together be like this day: nothing but blue skies.*

Ben

I sit with Terrence in a couple of white wooden folding chairs, off to the side, happy to be out of the spotlight, happy to watch Haley with her niece and nephew as they play with her family's fluffy gray cat in the yard. With tendrils of dark blond hair falling around her face, she doesn't realize that Sienna is subtly snapping pictures of them.

"Cora and Cole, huh?" Terrence asks like he's not sure of the niece and nephew's names—but I know he is.

"Yeah—what about them?" I ask, shifting my gaze his way.

He gives me a side-eye glance. "And Haley's sister is Hannah. And their mother, Nina, has a sister named Nan?"

Oh, okay, I get it now. "It's a family tradition, I guess." I smile slightly.

"So I guess we can expect a little Jack and Jill Page one of these days? Or Becky and Bobby? Susie and Sam?" He's clearly amused with himself.

I shoot him a pointed look and reply, "Not all family traditions are meant to last. No Jack and Jill for us." And don't get me wrong, I'm good with people who use the same letter for naming all their kids—but it might be a little much on every single branch of the family tree.

"Does Haley know that?"

I glance back at her, her white gown puddling around her as she kneels with the kids—then I refocus on Terrence. "We've never actually discussed it. But we agree on most things." And I can't think of much we *don't* agree on. Sure, we had a few rocky moments early in our relationship, and as she said in her vows, we're very different in ways—but we fit together like puzzle pieces.

Same with me and Terrence, kind of. Shoved together as college roommates as freshmen at the University of Cincinnati, we were two guys with nothing in common other than the same major—architecture. Terrence had grown up in the inner city; I'd come north from the hills of Kentucky. He was black; I was white. He had a chip on his shoulder; and me, I just laid low and kept to myself.

So we had nothing in common—but *everything* in common. We both grew up poor, with some hard losses along the way. We don't talk about it a lot, even now, ten years later—but it all bubbled to the surface late one night during that first semester. It was cold as hell, snow falling earlier than usual, and slick roads kept us both at the dorm for the weekend instead of heading home. Terrence offered me a beer, then another, and another—and we ended up spilling our guts to each other. That was when we went from being roommates to being best friends.

"You said some pretty serious stuff up there," he points out now, his tone less kidding and more circumspect. We also don't talk about the fact that I'm not a super-open guy, but I get why he's surprised. Over the years, he's evolved more than me in that way. And maybe I was surprised at myself during the wedding, too, but...

"I was asked to say how I felt about her, so I did. And now I'll be perfectly happy not to bare my soul again for the foreseeable future," I conclude with a quick grin, glad to have a buddy who gets me. And now a wife who gets me, too, even if in some entirely different ways. Puzzle pieces.

"A toast," Terrence says, lifting the glass of wine in his hand.

"You already did that." All the toasting and cake-cutting is already over with, and I'm ready for the honeymoon.

"This one's just between you and me," he replies. "A toast to you and Haley. Because I didn't expect you to find anyone, either." He cocks me a smart-aleck grin.

Which makes me let out a laugh. "You were worried I'd become the lifelong lonely man, Uncle Ben, who you'd have to include in your every family gathering for the rest of our lives, weren't you?"

He shrugs, and now we *both* laugh.

That's when I spot Pastor Tom's dog, Lulu, a pretty golden-doodle, in the near distance, galloping toward us.

"Hey girl," I say, reaching down to scratch her neck when she reaches us. "Are you supposed to be out running around on your own?" I grew up with dogs—my grandpa owned a kennel. So I never mind a chance encounter with Lulu, but there are leash laws, and I'm pretty sure our wedding is the last occasion when Tom would suddenly decide to turn her loose.

I don't have much time to ponder the issue, though,

before she gets bored with us and bolts off in another direction. A bad direction.

Before I can make a move, I hear the frightened screech of a cat as it darts under a hydrangea bush, followed by the equally panicked screech of my bride just before the dog streaks across the yard, a flowy white veil hanging from her jowls and trailing behind in the breeze.

I instinctively shove my wineglass into Terrence's hand and head toward Haley. She's on her feet now, looking horrified but none the worse for wear other than her hair being a little messier than before. "Are you okay?" I ask anyway.

She nods, but her eyes suggest differently.

I rub her shoulder and kiss her nose. "It's only a veil," I tell her. "And me chasing it down is gonna make for great pictures."

The idea makes her smile. She's right, I do balance her. And true to my prediction, I spot Sienna in my peripheral vision, just waiting for the comedy to ensue.

"So *you're* gonna be the one to chase the dog this time?" Haley asks softly, her voice at once wistful and teasing.

I smile, too, at the reminder of our first meeting, orchestrated by Aunt Nan and another dog I once knew.

Meanwhile, Pastor Tom has tuned in to what's happening and brings out his rare angry voice to call, "Lulu! Lulu, you come back here right now! Bad girl. Very bad girl."

As Lulu goes slinking toward the pond, Haley's veil whipping in the wind behind her, I put up a hand to stop him from stalking in her direction, suspecting she won't respond to his harsh tone—she's a fairly young dog and I'm betting he seldom sounds this upset with her. Perhaps arrogantly, I think

I have a better shot—plus I've promised Haley chasing pictures.

Reaching behind me, I grab up a strip of grilled chicken from a food table and walk calmly toward where Lulu crouches next to a bush by the water. "Hey Lulu," I call softly, "here, girl. Come and get some chicken. I'm sure you like chicken, don't you?"

Despite hearing the snaps of a camera nearby, I stay focused on my task: luring a white-tulle-wrapped dog. My entire boyhood was spent luring dogs—hence my confident taking-over of the situation. I get closer, cooing and baby-talking. "Who's a good girl? Lulu is a good girl. Come here, good girl."

It's working. She's realizing that I'm not mad—I'm just a guy who wants to give her a snack. I'm down on my knees now, putting myself on her level so I don't seem threatening. "Come here, girl. Bring me the veil and no one'll get hurt." I'm still using the baby voice on her, noticing the veil is wrapped around her in such a way that if she were wearing sunglasses, she'd look like the canine version of Audrey Hepburn in a convertible. She appears docile—just a girl out for a run with a swath of fluffy, white fabric.

I inch closer on my tux-clad knees, holding out the chicken. "Trade ya, Lulu. I know girls just wanna have fun, but I think your taste buds are gonna win out."

Slowly, still wearing the veil like an elaborate scarf, she catches sight—or maybe scent—of the chicken and comes toward me.

"That's right," I coo. "Good girl. Good girl."

And then she's gobbling down the chicken in my

outstretched palm as my other hand grabs firmly but gently onto her collar. Upon hearing soft applause, I look back to see that all the remaining guests have tuned in to the doggie drama.

"My knight in shining armor!" Haley calls as I unwind the veil from around Lulu's furry body.

Haley

It's kind of instinctive, isn't it, that if your bridal veil is ripped off your head by a renegade dog, you think you *must* rescue it and put it back on? And yet, even after Ben's skilled heroism, I leave it off. The guests are mostly gone, and while it felt jarring for a moment, the veil theft simply added some excitement to the day. "And I got some amazing shots," Sienna tells me. She loves a dramatic turn like that at a wedding.

"Has anyone seen the cat?" I ask, looking around. Mostly an indoor kitty, Puff generally stays close when let outside, so perhaps the fright he suffered is the bigger issue here.

"I got him!" Cora calls, hauling the cat in a position that looks uncomfortable for him—but I'm glad to see he hasn't taken off for parts unknown. Pastor Tom has locked Lulu back in his house, so the coast is clear.

"Good job, Cora," I tell her. "Will you bring him to me?"

We got Puff as a kitten when I was fifteen, making him ten now, and I'm suddenly feeling sentimental, remembering how he used to sleep with me when I was a teenager, and how, as a kitten, he would wake me up by walking across my body with soft, gentle paws. I've had my own apartment for a few years, but my parents' house has always been *home*. And now that I have a husband, something about that feels a little different. More like I'm moving out than when I actually moved out—even though I'll be a mile away in the very same apartment, just with Ben now. And we're already saving to buy a house, so the meaning of *home* for me has no choice but to change.

After Cora hefts the cat onto the table where I'm sitting, I lean over and touch my nose to his, and he lets me. We linger like that—perhaps he senses the gravity of the moment.

Running my fingers through his fur, I whisper, "I'm gonna miss you, buddy. I mean, I'll still see you a lot, but it might not be the same." I sometimes house-sit for my parents when they travel, and if I'm sick, I've been known to come home and let my mother take care of me for a few days. And those things won't happen anymore—I have someone new to take care of me.

My sister, however, doesn't get this. "You realize you haven't lived here for years, right?" she says behind me.

I keep my eyes on the cat. "I know, but still..." I look up at her. And *then* she gets it.

She rests a hand on my shoulder. "Life moves fast sometimes, doesn't it?"

"Just when you think it's not," I say, remembering the woe of pre-Ben heartbreaks that had me certain I'd be sad forever, "then it does. In good ways. Great ways. But I'm just realizing that I'm officially not a little girl anymore."

"I once felt that way, too. But then I had my own little girl—and it's just another new part of the journey. Just think, one of these days, you'll waltz into the bakery some morning and tell me you and Ben are expecting! And Cora and Cole will get a little cousin!"

Her eyes are all alight, but I still say, "Slow down there, Quickdraw. Today just let me enjoy being a bride and saying a ceremonial goodbye to the cat."

We laugh, and as if on cue, Ben parts from talking with my dad and comes over to ask, "Ready to go?"

Part of me hates for our glorious wedding day to end, but I'm also ready to start that next chapter I talked about during the vows. Hannah is right—there's so much more wonderful stuff ahead. So I nod, take his hand, and stand up, ready to step into my new life.

"Oh, there you two are!"

We both turn to find Aunt Nan, decked out in all her wedding finery, tips of silvery hair peeking out from beneath that periwinkle hat. I instinctively go to hug her, but realize her hands are full—she's holding a beautifully wrapped gift.

"I wanted to give you my wedding present before you leave."

I smile, then glance toward the pile of gifts near the back door, which Mom and Dad will deliver to our apartment while we're honeymooning in Hawaii. "Oh, they go on that table," I tell her, "and we'll open them when we get back."

"I know that, dear, but I need to give you this one personally. And you won't open it when you get back because it comes with special instructions not to, so you'll need to set it aside, apart from the rest."

Ben and I exchange glances. "You're giving us a gift we can't open?" he asks.

"Exactly." She adds a succinct nod.

I purse my lips in confusion. "If we can't open it, then why...or what...is the point?"

I don't mean that snidely, and the rich sound of her laughter reassures me she knows that. "You can open it *eventually*," she explains. "But you're to save it until you have your first big disagreement."

Another quick tossing of looks takes place between Ben and me, her words opening a floodgate of thoughts. *Maybe we won't have disagreements. And even if we do—everyone does, right?—I don't necessarily want to think about that now, on our special day. And leave it to Aunt Nan to give us the most unique of gifts, one we can't open until something goes wrong.*

Though I keep all this to myself, it must be written all over my face, since she answers me anyway. "No marriage is trouble-free. If it is, then someone's holding something back. No two people see the world exactly the same, but marriage isn't *supposed* to be perfect. We grow through conflict and adversity."

At this, my eyes bolt open wider. "Conflict and adversity? This is my wedding day, Aunt Nan!" I can't believe she's raining on my perfect blue-sky day with conflict and adversity! "I always thought you and Uncle Philip were happy together," I go on, incredulous.

"Oh, we were, my dear, we were," she says on a carefree laugh. Even though I'm not finding any of this very funny. "But again, no marriage is without its troubles. And this box will make that easier when the time comes."

And then the gift is in my hands. About a foot square, it's wrapped in lovely, patterned, cream-colored paper and tied with an elaborate lace ribbon, sprigs of off-white silk roses tucked in around the bow. "It's...beautiful, Aunt Nan," I have to admit, though I'm suddenly wary of it somehow.

"Well, I thought since it might stay wrapped a while," she says on a wink, "it should be pleasant to look at."

Then she tells us she loves us both and wishes us all the happiness in the world. "And I'll see you after you get back. You'll call me first thing, right? I want to hear you went surfing and learned to hula dance."

But my mind is still on the emotionally-heavy gift I'm holding, even as we all laugh at her last words. "I'm pretty sure we'll keep it simpler," I tell her, trying to focus on the conversation, "spending days on the beach or exploring the island, and spending nights...well, honeymooning." More light laughter fills the air, but it hits me just then that if Aunt Nan ever went to Hawaii, she would totally take surfing lessons and hula classes.

My thoughts continue to swirl, even after she turns to go. And when Ben takes the box from me a moment later, carrying it toward the gift table anyway, I touch his arm. "Shouldn't we hang on to it, keep it apart from the others?"

He stops, looks uncertain. "I could put it in the car trunk—that way we'll remember not to open it." Then he casts a speculative glance down. "Or...we could just open it now."

I raise my eyebrows, aghast. "Why would we do that?"

"Well, aren't you curious what's inside? I mean, what on earth could she think is going to solve any potential problem that ever crops up between us?"

I release a melancholy sigh. "I know she meant well, but it's horrible to have to think about that on our wedding day."

"Right. And if we don't open it now, don't you think it'll

sort of...hang over our heads? We'll be waiting for this big, awful moment of deciding to open it?"

I see why he's tempted, and yet... "What if the mystery gift in this box *is* the perfect thing to make everything better whenever we have that first big fight? And if we don't have it to open, it can't fix whatever the problem is."

He tilts his head, then continues trying to justify opening it. "Well, after we see what it is, we can tuck it away and save it for that moment."

I shake my head, though. "What if it doesn't work that way? What if it only solves the problem if you open it when it's happening? Otherwise, she wouldn't have told us to wait."

"I'm not sure that makes sense," he argues. "If we see it's something that solves a problem, won't it solve it just as well when we actually have one?"

This is getting a little too complicated for the moment, so I insist, "We should honor the intention of the gift and wait."

But Ben isn't convinced. "I'm afraid just knowing it's sitting there, unopened, could drive us crazy." Though he challenges me with raised eyebrows. "Are you saying the anticipation, the mystery of it, isn't killing you already?"

I look at the box in his hands. He's right, it is. "But we still can't."

A cute, crafty smile unfurls across his handsome face before he suggests, "Hey, maybe this qualifies as our first disagreement. Instant permission to open."

Maybe I should just give in, end the suspense. But again, I'm a little afraid of it now.

Aunt Nan would hate me feeling this way about her gift, but even as we both stare down at it, I can't help wondering:

Is marriage going to be as hard as Aunt Nan just said? Is this box a warning about bad times to come?

I narrow my gaze on him and plant my fists on my hips. "Ben, this is Aunt Nan we're talking about. If this is the one thing she asks of us, we have to do it. I mean, without Aunt Nan, we never would have met."

2

Before...

Haley

Aunt Nan and I stand next to Uncle Philip's gravestone, admiring our handiwork. It's spring—the sun is shining for the first time after days of drizzle—and the pink hyacinth bulbs we planted at the base of the stone last fall are in bloom. In addition to the silk flowers in the vases on either side of the stone that bears both their names even though she's not there yet, we've just placed small pots of tulips at both ends, as well.

The flowers are beautiful, but the real party, unmistakably, takes place in the branches of the friendly elm tree above, several of which stretch out over the grave, conveniently at eye level.

When Aunt Nan chose the spot after her husband's passing three years ago, I feared bird poop, but she chose it because he loved trees and she thought she might hang a wind chime. Now *three* sets of wind chimes tinkle harmoniously in the breeze, but somehow the use of the tree has evolved even more. It started one year at Christmas when she got the idea to tie red ribbons among the branches and hang some ornaments. It looked so pretty that now we "re-ribbon" the tree for every season, adding other hanging seasonal decorations, too. Today we've decked out the branches in spring pastels and lace.

An extensively decorated grave says way more about the person doing the decorating than the person buried there, though I've heard it questioned why people do it. For Aunt Nan, it started as a distraction from her loss. Uncle Philip had long suffered coronary issues, but that didn't make it any less heartbreaking when he died. Keeping the grave looking festive honored his memory—and gave her a hobby. For me, it's my way of helping her grieve.

I grieved, too, of course—I was always close with both of them. They had no children of their own, and they loved babysitting Hannah and me when we were kids. Hannah is a few years older, though, and as she grew up and got into other things, I still adored spending a snowy weekend or a lazy Saturday night at Aunt Nan and Uncle Philip's, playing board games or working jigsaw puzzles by a roaring fire.

Yet my grief passed a lot faster than my aunt's, of course. I came with her in the beginning to help her feel supported, like she wasn't alone. Now I come...well, for the same reasons, I guess. But it's grown into a habit, a thing we do together.

Sometimes we take walks around the cemetery before or after our grave-tending, and frankly, I find it a little maudlin to be so surrounded by death. But it helps Aunt Nan feel closer to Uncle Philip—even as, at the very same time, she tells me she knows his soul isn't really here. "If he were to pop in, though, I'd certainly want the place looking nice," she told me once with a wink. No taking a walk on the agenda today, though—the sun is starting to dry things, but there's still a damp chill to the air.

A sleek, shiny black sedan glides past us as we stand next to the grave, directly beside one of the twisty, winding cemetery lanes. I glance up as the car slows down about thirty yards away and eases to a stop, then I return my attention to a yellow gingham ribbon tied to a branch and in need of a little straightening.

"Oh my," Aunt Nan croons softly.

I peek over at her, pretty sure she's not just admiring my bow adjustment, then follow her eyes to the stopped car. Or, more precisely, to the man who just exited it. With dark hair and a chiseled jawline, he's remarkably handsome and clearly well-groomed, but he strikes me as austere. Wearing a black business suit—as sleek as the car—I find him intimidatingly attractive, even from that distance. The only soft thing about him is the fact that he's accompanied by a cute little Yorkie on a hot pink—decidedly *not* austere—leash. The cute dog looks out of place with him.

I shift my glance to Aunt Nan. "What?"

"He's a handsome one."

Yeah, I noticed that. But so what? "I suppose."

"You should go talk to him."

Lowering my chin, I flash a pointed a look in her direction. "Surely you're kidding."

"Not at all. He's handsome and looks like a man who knows what he's about."

I've never before heard Aunt Nan describe anyone that way—but then the proverbial lightbulb clicks on over my head. "Oh. Oh, I get it now." It's about my last boyfriend. Well, maybe even the last *two*.

Kirby was a wannabe singer-songwriter who Aunt Nan said from the beginning had his heads in the clouds too much for a girl like me. I disagreed, because my head is sometimes in the clouds, too—but in the end she was right. I was much more settled and responsible than him, and he broke my heart by whisking off to New York to pursue his dreams, with the parting words, "You're a cool chick and I'd ask you to come with me, but you seem real into that bakery thing, so I figure you're stuck here." Yeah. Not stuck. I'm an entrepreneur and business owner, thankyouverymuch.

And then came Austin, an art professor at a local university. We liked the same things and we're both creative types. We went to museums and bookstores together, and watched art house movies. He was that guy I could sit with at opposite ends of a sofa on a rainy day, both of us reading a book but sharing the same cozy throw blanket—feeling together even while we indulged in something separate. He seemed so much more grounded than Kirby and I fell in love quick. And things were grand...until I found out my boyfriend had a girlfriend—one who wasn't me. Which meant I wasn't actually his girlfriend.

Crushed for the second time in a year, I decided—we all did, my whole family including Aunt Nan—that I should take a break from dating and focus on other things. And that's what I've been doing for months now. Focusing on the bakery—we've done some adorable redecorating—and focusing on just figuring out who I am. The truth I've had to admit to myself is that I really just don't like arty films that much—I just liked the *idea* of them. And that I probably shouldn't hitch my star to someone who has aspirations elsewhere because I do love the business my sister and I have quickly made into a vibrant part of our community.

So all things considered, I'm a little surprised Aunt Nan is suddenly suggesting I go throw myself at a stranger. "What's gotten into you?" I ask. "I'm choosing to be happily single right now, if you recall. A decision you were very on board with until this moment."

She shrugs in her easy Aunt Nan way. "Time passes, things change."

I narrow my gaze on her skeptically. This guy—though I've only looked at him for about a second—is not my kind of guy. He looks so corporate and well-put-together that I'm almost as intimidated by his style and serious nature as I am by his good looks. My first impression is that he's someone who never smiles. And I have no idea why that dog has a pink leash, but I almost suspect it's borrowed since this is *not* a man who picks out a pink leash.

"Things haven't changed for me," I told her. "I think it's wise for me to stay out of the dating pool for a while. I was drowning there, and it's nice not to be in the throes of heart-break for a change." I cast a sidelong glance at Austere Man. He stands before a grave marker, peering somberly down. The Yorkie seems less interested, pulling uselessly against the leash. "And even if I *were* interested in dating right now, this guy? What on earth about him says approachable to you? Because I'm getting the opposite vibe."

She appears undaunted by my arguments. "I think you're being quick to judge. And there's a time for all things. A time for not dating—and a time for moving on and taking chances and being bold. Life is short."

I just look at her. This is an entire about face. But her last words hit me, reminding me where we are and why. Maybe this is about Uncle Philip and wishing she'd had more years with him. And *whatever* it's about, it's because she wants me to find love. Which softens my stance a little. Even though I still have no intention of walking up to this man and starting a conversation.

"Even so," I say a bit more softly, "I'm pretty sure a cemetery is the last place one should approach a person and attempt to flirt. People come here to indulge in private feelings, and they expect to be left alone to do it."

Nonetheless, she argues. "I wouldn't mind if someone spoke to me here. In fact, people have. People sometimes stop to admire the tree." She takes on a gentle look of pride. Then glances again toward Austere Man. "In fact, it might just make his day. Human interaction is a wonderful thing—it brings out the best in most people."

I say nothing. She's wearing me out, frankly. It's unlike her to be so pushy about something like this. As a general rule, we're not a family of women who go out chasing men. If any one of us has ever been a man chaser, it's me—so if *I* think this seems like a bad idea, then it's a bad idea. "This is a bad idea," I tell her.

"No, it's a lovely idea. Just a simple hello."

"And then what? What on earth is it you think I should say to him? While he's standing next to the grave of someone he loved, no less."

"Ask him what kind of dog that is."

I roll my eyes. "It's a Yorkie."

She sighs, as if I'm slow on the uptake. "*You* know it's a Yorkie and *I* know it's a Yorkie, but *he* doesn't know we know it's a Yorkie. Blame me. Tell him your aunt wants to know." Then she makes a shooing motion at me, like I'm a fly on her picnic food. "Go on," she says. Then she smiles. "Just do it. It'll be fun."

I'm actually taking a few steps backward in his general direction, from the shooing, even as I flash looks of doubt and contempt. But I'm not sure if the doubt and contempt are for her or for me, since for some reason I seem to be moving toward him.

Her smile widens, and she's nodding at what she sees as her success. "There now—keep going." She's lowered her voice, though, so he won't hear.

I turn to walk his way, one thought in my head. *Am I really doing this?* But then I see that he's left the graveside to head back toward his car.

I spin toward Aunt Nan. "He's leaving," I say in a loud whisper.

"Then you'd better hurry," she loud-whispers back.

Another eye roll from me. Again, at myself as much as her, for being manipulated into such madness for no other reason than thinking it's sweet that she wants me to find romance.

I begin walking faster now, trudging up the slight incline

that lies between Austere Man and me, because if I'm doing this, I have to do it—and once he sees me coming, the space between us only grows more awkward while I'm getting there.

He opens the passenger door and seems to be fiddling with the dog's leash before putting her back in the car. Although he hasn't looked up, I assume he's aware of me as I get closer and closer. Yet an acknowledgement of some kind would be nice—so that I don't feel as totally silly as I'm beginning to.

None comes, though, and then there I am, nearly at the back bumper of his car. So I say, "Hi. My aunt was wondering—"

He flinches, because I've clearly caught him completely off guard—and two horrible things happen simultaneously: He spins around, bringing an expensive-looking shoe down into a ridiculously-deep mud puddle, and the dog, now undone from the leash, darts.

"Bella!" he calls after the dog. "Bella, come back here!" And as he prepares to give chase, he steps completely out of his shoe, which remains in the mud.

So *I* give chase. I take off and chase that dog with fear and dread and passion in my heart. Because it's my fault she's loose, and if she gets lost and can't find her way back, it's on me. This guy was just minding his own business, visiting the cemetery with his Yorkie, and I've come along and created chaos.

The chase also comes with the need to escape *him*.

And that shoe in the mud.

And the look of bewilderment on his perfect face.

And the entire mess I've somehow created with a mere half-sentence.

I'm running—trundling really—awkwardly over hill and dale, catching glimpses of Bella bounding between one tombstone and next, behind bushes and into brush. Why did we have to bury Uncle Philip at such a foliage-rich cemetery? I occasionally slip or slide on wet grass, but I keep going. One time I fall—and I catch sight of a grass stain on my jeans, but still I persist. "Bella—here, Bella," I call gently.

I have no idea if Austere Man has followed or if he's still dealing with the shoe issue—dear God, I've single-handedly lost his dog *and* ruined his shoes—and I'm actually hoping for the latter. Maybe she'd be more likely to come to *him*, but I feel like a dolt and now prefer to stay as far away from him as possible.

Pretty soon, I realize that Bella thinks we're playing—she repeatedly lets me get within a few yards of her and then takes off again. Then at other times she disappears entirely, scaring me to death, making me think she's gone, that I've let the serious man's dog get away, that she'll be frightened and alone and lost and I'll never get a good night's sleep again.

"Bella, pleeeease," I beg this dog I don't even know. "Please let me catch you. Please let me return you to your owner guy." She's only a few feet away, and I approach her ever-so-gingerly, her leash just within my reach—yet there she goes, off to the races again.

When I lose sight of her completely, I find myself running this way and that, at a loss, near tears. I can't lose this dog. I just can't. I have to find her.

That's when I catch a glimpse of her galloping full speed

away from me across a stretch of cemetery toward...Austere Man. She and I have made a big circle somehow and I now hear him cooing, "Here, girl. Yes, there you are—there you are. Good girl. What a good girl." He stoops down so the dog can leap into his arms, and of course she's wet and muddy now and so his expensive-looking suit and tie are wet and muddy now, too. Then I notice he's still one-shoed. But the main thing I'm aware of—besides my ongoing horror and humiliation—is the cute, affectionate voice he's using with her. "Such a good girl. A wet girl, but a good girl. You gave me a scare there." He's petting and hugging and nuzzling her. It's wildly endearing and my heart swells. He's seeming less austere all the time.

Which kind of sucks for me. Since I'm pretty sure I'm not his dream girl. Especially as I come trudging toward the car breathless, dirt on my hands and jeans, and I catch a glimpse of grass stain streaked across the once-cute T-shirt I'm wearing, pale yellow and emblazoned with a daisy design. My hair was up in a fun, messy bun when this started and now most of it is blowing haphazardly in my face and probably every other direction as well.

"I'm so sorry," I say. I'm past the hope of making any reasonable impression on him—I just need to express my sincere apology. "I didn't mean to sneak up on you. Or scare your dog away. Or make you step in mud." I sigh, then lower my eyes. It's a lot.

"I'm just glad you found her."

Okay, I wouldn't exactly say I found her—I would say I'm lucky she ran in a big circle. And it's not exactly forgiveness or absolution. But I'll take it. Even though he sounds slightly stiffer talking to me than to the dog.

"She's really cute," I remark. It's all I got. "And a fast runner." I'm going for a joke there—but it doesn't land; no smile. Guess I was right—he's not a guy who smiles.

"She belongs to my girlfriend. She would have killed me if I'd lost her."

Ah, okay. But not a big surprise at this point. Just a little more bitter icing on a rotten cake. "I'm sure." I think I'll change the subject. But it doesn't help much since all the subjects we have between us are unpleasant ones. "Um, about your shoe." It's out of the mud now, but covered in brown slime. "Can I...reimburse you?"

He shakes his head. "Oh—no. That was *my* fault. You didn't put the mud there." What I hear is: *The rest of it was your doing, but not the mud.*

I feel beyond awkward and suspect I'm making weird faces and odd gestures as I say in a fumbling way, "Is there... anything I can...do? To help? Again, I'm so sorry."

He shakes his head. Still no smile, but he replies, "Nothing to be sorry for. I should have been more aware." Again, no blame —he's a gentleman. Just not a happy, smiling one. But I can't fault him. He's had a fright over the dog *and* ruined a probably pricy pair of shoes. He'll have to drive wearing only a sock on his gas pedal foot. And that suit will need to go straight to the cleaners.

"I hope you weren't heading anywhere important." I bite my lip, praying for that—because I've already messed up enough for him.

He shakes his head as he loads Bella into the car again,

quickly shutting the door behind her this time. "No—just on my way home from work. Picked the dog up from the groomer's and thought I'd make a quick stop at the cemetery."

Oh, even better news—Bella just came from the groomer's. Now that I think about it, she might have been sporting a little bright pink bow on her head when this started, but I'm pretty sure it's gone now. He's limping around the car toward the driver's side, shoe in hand, as I offer up, "Well, I hope your evening gets better from here."

"Couldn't get much worse," he mumbles—then pauses before opening the door. "Um, what were you saying about... your aunt or something—when the dog bolted?"

"Oh." That seems so long ago. I point vaguely toward where Aunt Nan is still standing, after all this, next to Uncle Philip's grave and say, "She was wondering what kind of dog Bella is."

"A Yorkie," he replies.

"I thought so," I tell him with a weak attempt at a smile.

"Take care," he says—in that quick *I'm off* sort of way, and then he's behind the wheel, door slamming, driving into the distance. The lanes in the cemetery circle around so that he doesn't have to drive back past me—which I'll consider a small blessing.

I'm a little shellshocked as I make my way back toward Aunt Nan. It started out as such a normal afternoon. "Well," I announce as I get nearer, "being bold really went well, didn't it?"

She's biting her lip, and I spy some combination of guilt and amusement in her expression. "Cheer up," she tells me.

"We had an extra little adventure today. And you have a funny story to tell Hannah at the bakery tomorrow."

"Oh yeah—hilarious," I say dryly. "And thank you for running to my aid, by the way."

"What could I do?" she says with a shrug. "I'm an old lady."

I roll my eyes.

"Come here—there's a twig in your hair," she says, reaching to pull it out.

"Of course there is," I mumble. "Why would I expect any less?"

"Any sparks?" she asks.

And at this, I crack up laughing. Because it's truly the funniest thing I've heard all day. And I suppose I need the release at this point. "I'm not sure he's the twigs-in-hair, grass-stains-on-clothes type. Oh, and he has a girlfriend, by the way." It hits me then that I was right—he hadn't picked out a pink leash.

Aunt Nan gives yet another shrug. "It was worth a try. Ya win some, ya lose some. *Que sera sera.*"

Easy for her to say. Because somehow what stays with me is how sweet he was with the dog when she finally came back to him. And how sweet he *wasn't* with me—again, not that I can blame him. And that I envy his girlfriend a little. Because he's probably sweet to *her*. Which is exactly the sort of feeling I didn't have before Aunt Nan practically shoved me up that hill. Which is why I didn't want to go. I didn't want to know he could be anything I want if I can't have him. And he was so devastatingly handsome. Even more than I'd realized from a distance. Another thing I wish I hadn't noticed.

None of it matters. He isn't my type. And he's taken anyway. And I'll never see him again. I just hope he doesn't stay on my mind. Because sometimes it's that simple—one little encounter stays on your mind and makes you think you want something you don't have.

3

Ben

Just like every time I go to the cemetery to visit Gramps' grave lately, I glance over at the resting place decorated with ribbons and flowers as I pass by. It's September and the leaves on the branches draping over it have turned a pale yellow, but the ladies make their decorations show up amidst fall gold by using orange and maroon-colored bows. Little craft store scarecrows bob from the lowest tree branch, as well, and an array of pumpkins are grouped at the base of the gravestone.

It's been five months since that crazy day I met the younger grave decorator and Bella ran away. I know because the grave was decked out in Easter colors then, and because that was the day I decided to break up with Taryn.

The decision wasn't connected to the event—but in a way, maybe it was. I shouldn't have had the dog with me, but

Taryn was famous for last minute texts dropping her responsibilities on me.

That day it was: *Need you to pick up Bella at groomer's by 5. Can't get out of work.*

No *thanks* or *sorry* or *please* or the consideration to wonder if *I* could get out of work.

It wasn't the first time, and maybe I made too much of it, but when all was said and done, I couldn't help thinking it was ultimately *her* fault those frantic few minutes with the runaway pup happened, her fault my new Cole Haans bit the dust after three whole wearings, and her fault I wasn't very nice to a woman who just happened to approach me at the wrong moment.

We just weren't right for each other and the sad truth is that I miss Bella a lot more than Taryn, and I'm glad I didn't let her pressure me into moving in together.

As for the grave decorator, I've kept an eye out for her here all summer—but we must keep different schedules. I wasn't at my best that day, and I've felt like a jerk about it ever since.

I've stayed mildly intrigued by a woman who, without a thought, went sprinting through the cemetery after a dog she had no connection to. I've wanted to apologize and thank her. I've wanted to explain that I'm not some prima donna dude too good to chase the dog myself—but the shoe thing really threw me. Hell, it *all* threw me. I don't even know if I'd recognize her if I saw her. The whole event happened so quickly.

"What's up, Grandpa?" I say as I exit the car and approach the grave. Sometimes I talk to Grandpa Ed when I'm here; sometimes I don't. I'm not actually a big grave-talking guy by nature—but it's a thing Grandpa used to do himself. When I was a kid, we visited the cemetery in my rural hometown weekly. First stop, Grandma. Second stop, Mom and Dad.

Gramps carried on big conversations with them all like he was writing a letter or leaving a phone message. "Well, the transmission went out on the pickup. Junior at the garage says it'll take two weeks to get parts, so Ben and me are in the Ford today. He made all A's on his report card again—even in science, which was worrying him. Does us all proud, I tell ya. Thawin' some pork chops for dinner. Gonna bread 'em and fry 'em up while Ben makes the mashed potatoes. Gonna start some brown beans soakin' tonight, too—pot o' those'll make us a week's worth o' suppers."

Then he'd nudge my shoulder and tell me to go on and say something myself. So I learned to say the same sorts of things. "Wrecked my bike—made Gramps mad, but it's not like I did it on purpose. I like all my teachers this year, except for Mrs. Sebree in math. We're learning about the westward migration in history class right now from Mr. Veigel."

I'm pretty firmly in the camp of not thinking the person in the grave is really there in spirit. But I go, and I talk a little, because whether or not there's an afterlife, it was important to Gramps.

And today I'm in a pretty good mood. "Meeting Terrence to pitch plans for a skyscraper to a developer in a little while," I tell the gravestone. "Just right up the street." I live down the hill in Covington, an old city that sits directly across the Ohio River from downtown Cincinnati where my firm is located, but the developer's office is in Lakeside Park, not far from the cemetery. "I didn't expect the opportunity this soon, but the boss liked our designs better than anyone else's, so he tapped us for the pitch." It's a first for us—being the key voices on a pitch, especially one this big. "If this goes our way, it's gonna be *huge*. The kind of huge you and I used to talk about. Living-the-dream huge. Changing-the-skyline huge."

That's when it hits me to be a little nervous. Up to now, I've only been excited—but damn, I don't want to blow this. I want to know I'd have made Grandpa Ed proud. I want the chance to do the thing I've always dreamed of—alter the city skyline. That's always been my measure of success, since the first days I realized I wanted to be an architect. Adding something to the skyline is as permanent a mark as I can hope to make on the world.

Most people might just see Cincinnati as one more generic Midwestern city—but for a poor Kentucky orphan farm boy...well, for me, it's my New York. My L.A. My Chicago. Gramps lived there as a young man, and a framed picture of the Roebling Suspension Bridge spanning the Ohio, with the city sparkling on the other side, hung over the couch in our farmhouse when I was a kid. Cincinnati became my "city on the hill" and getting an apartment right across the river after college, with Gramps coming up to live with me, was my first step to claiming it. Getting a job there a few months later was my next step. And this meeting today is a chance for the whole enchilada—a way to leave a part of myself there that no one can take away for a very long time.

It's a pretty fall morning—warm for just past ten—and I stopped at the cemetery because I'm early and it's on the way. But as I take another look at my grandpa's name on the stone, I can't deny feeling like he's with me a little, cheering me on, telling me I can do this—just like I've done everything else I've set out to in my career so far. "This is just the next step, Gramps. I'm only sorry you won't be here to see that building rise up into the sky."

Exiting the cemetery a few minutes later, I spare another glance to the heavily decorated grave as I go back by. For the first time, I even stop, roll down my window, and take a closer look. There are two names on the double-heart marble headstone, but only one has a death date filled in: Philip Fitzsimmons.

"You must have been a hell of a guy," I say—since apparently I'm all about talking to gravestones today. But mainly I'm still wishing I'd run into the young woman—his granddaughter maybe?—who so diligently cares for the grave. No, wait—she'd said the older woman was her aunt—she must be a niece. Regardless, it's hard to look at that grave and not feel a lot of love there.

I take a left out onto the road, and a quick mile later I find street parking in a quaint retail and restaurant district just a couple of blocks long, plunked down in an otherwise mostly residential community. The developer's office is tucked into a group of refurbished storefronts that houses a micro-brewery, fashion boutique, and sandwich shop.

I'm still early, and I could use a shot of caffeine, so I scoop up my briefcase and start toward a coffee shop I spotted before parking. At the corner past the boutique, I hit the button for a *walk* light to cross the street.

As cars *whoosh* past while I wait for the light to change, I hear a clatter on the sidewalk behind me just before someone loudly exclaims, "Oh no! What a clumsy thing to do."

I turn to see an older silver-haired woman peering down at a plum-colored handbag on the sidewalk, its contents scattered. She meets my gaze with a bereft sigh. "I'm so sorry to bother you, but could you possibly lend me a hand? My knees aren't what they used to be."

"Of course," I say, lowering my briefcase to the concrete, then stooping to collect her belongings.

"Darn thing just got away from me," she says. "Practically leaped out of my hands."

Still gathering her stuff into the leather purse, I glance up with a small smile. "They can do that, I'm told." I don't even know what I mean by that, but I'm just being nice. See, this is how I usually act toward strangers—as opposed to how I behaved with Grave-Decorating Girl. I find myself vaguely wishing she could see that I'm a decent guy.

When I've awkwardly refilled the bag, I stand up and pass it to the silver-haired woman. "Here you go."

"Thank you so much, young man."

"It's no problem." I pick up my briefcase and turn back toward the street—just as the *don't walk* sign goes solid red and cars start whizzing past again.

"Oh dear, I've made you miss your light," she says.

And I laugh. "No worries—it'll change again."

"Where are you crossing the street to?" she asks in a friendly way.

I point toward the coffee shop. "Grabbing a cup of coffee before a meeting."

Her expression changes into that of someone who has a secret. "Oh, you don't want to get your coffee *there*."

That catches me off guard. "I don't?"

She shakes her head.

"Why not?"

"Well, it's not that there's anything *wrong* with their coffee," she says as if confiding in me, "but the best coffee in the neighborhood is on this side." She points up the street behind her. "At the bakery."

Before I can form a response, she hooks her arm through mine and says, "Here, I'll show you," and begins leading me down the street.

"That's nice of you, but not necessary," I tell her.

"Think nothing of it—I'm headed in that direction already."

I'm not going to be rude enough to pull away—I just hope this bakery of hers isn't far because my meeting is a block in the opposite direction in twenty minutes and I can't be late.

Fortunately, she says, "Right here," a moment a later, stopping us in front of an old-fashioned storefront that's been updated with a pink-and-black-striped awning, and according to the pink script on the window is the *Two Sisters Bakery*.

"Thank you again for your help with my purse." She has a sweet smile, this persistent older woman.

"Happy to help. And thank *you* for the, uh, recommendation." I motion toward the door, then head inside.

It's as cute on the inside as out, with black café tables, and chairs sporting pink tufted seats. Glass-front counters display colorfully-decorated donuts, cookies, and cupcakes.

My eyes are drawn to a pretty blond woman in a pink

apron rounding the counter toward the only other customers currently in the place, a mother with a teenage boy with Down Syndrome. She holds out a cookie. "Have a triple chocolate chunk for the road, Graham, on the house."

The middle-aged mom kindly balks with a friendly smile. "You won't stay in business long if you keep giving away your wares."

The bakery girl shrugs, smiles. "You guys are my best customers." Then she winks at Graham. "Besides, it's the last one on the tray, so you'd be doing me a favor by taking it off my hands."

"If you insist," Graham cheerfully replies, taking the cookie.

They all exchange thank yous and goodbyes, and I hold the door open as the two exit. Letting it fall shut, my eyes land on a framed piece of wall art that says *It's Cupcake O'Clock Somewhere*. For me, it's coffee o'clock, so I step up to the counter.

Haley

"Hi—can I help you?" The words are out of my mouth before I really focus on the man across from me. It's been months, but I'd know him anywhere. Same dark, sleek suit, same well-groomed hair and devastatingly handsome face. I try not to let it show in my expression.

"I'll have a cup of coffee," he says, then offers up a small grin. "It comes highly recommended."

Okay, wait a minute. Maybe I'm wrong. Because this guy is smiling. And the guy I met didn't seem to possess that particular skill. Now I'm puzzled. For more reasons than one. The other reason is: "It does?"

He raises his eyebrows. "I was about to cross the street to Perk Me Up, but a lady grabbed my arm and insisted I come here instead. Wow me." A good-natured laugh leaves him, and I'm still trying to wrap my head around this new and improved version of the guy I met in the cemetery. The guy who, like it or not, has stayed on my mind. Partially because of the embarrassment. And partially because...well, I hate to chalk it up to his good looks, but something about him held my interest, austere or not.

"I'll do my best," I assure him as I turn to pour the coffee.

The truth is, I've looked for him every time I've been to the cemetery since then. And the further truth is that I've gone to the cemetery more often than usual. Yes, to help Aunt Nan keep Uncle Philip's display tidy, but it's also a good, quiet place to walk or read a book. There are even park benches here and there—and I guess I suddenly decided it wasn't so maudlin, after all. But he never showed up, and now, here he is, out of the blue when I least expect it.

When Hannah walks up next to me in a pink Two Sisters apron that matches my own, toting a sleeve of paper coffee cups, I say very softly, through clenched teeth, "That's the guy."

She clenches her teeth in return to mock me as she asks, "What guy?"

"The cemetery guy." I told her about the whole crazy event, of course. Aunt Nan was right—it was a good story. So good that most of the people in my life have heard it now.

"The one-shoed, dog guy?"

"Yes." We're both still speaking through clenched teeth and not looking at each other. Music playing through strategically-placed speakers makes the secret conversation feasible.

Though now she unclenches to say, "Wow." Then steals a glance over her shoulder. "*Wow.*" This second wow is a *you-were-right-he's-hot* wow. She's my sister, so I speak her language.

"I know, right?" I blow out a sigh, thinking. I don't want to be fanning myself over how attractive this guy is any more than I wanted to approach him that day. "I still blame Aunt Nan for all of this."

Hannah shrugs. "That's neither here nor there—you still have to serve the man his coffee."

And he probably thinks I'm the slowest coffee pourer ever. I turn back to the counter and set the cup on top, telling him, "I hope it lives up to the hype."

He lifts his gaze agreeably from the wares in our glass-front counter back to me. This seems like a problem. If he stayed on my mind when he was more of a scowler, how much real estate is he going to take up in my brain now that he's friendly?

"I've been standing here getting tempted by your donuts and cupcakes," he admits.

I rub my palms together like a cartoon villain. "Then our evil plan is working."

He grins.

I do, too.

This is a nightmare.

"I'll take...two jelly donuts."

Two. *Like for you and your girlfriend?* "Fine choice," I say instead. "A classic. For here or to go?" I'm still pleasant, but I just remembered the girlfriend and now I'm a little sad inside.

"To go."

"Special occasion?" I blurt out unplanned. It's kind of a stupid question—it's two donuts, not a bottle of champagne—and nosy to boot. But nosiness is a bad habit of mine, and I'm suddenly a little desperate to extend the conversation, not let him get away just yet. And a little desperate to know if there's still a girlfriend. After all, I've been waiting to run into him again for months.

I can tell the question throws him a little, but he stays polite and gracious. "Actually, a friend and I have an important business meeting in a few minutes. If it goes our way, we can celebrate with donuts." Only then he looks a little doubtful, much more like the unhappy guy I remember. "But if it *doesn't* go our way..."

"Then they become conciliatory donuts. A donut makes everything better," I point out. "It's kind of perfect for any occasion."

He laughs softly as I begin packing his donuts. "True enough. I guess that's why I'm getting them. It's hard to resist a good donut, not matter *what* mood you're in."

I smile and tell him, "I like the way you think." Am I flirting? I don't mean to be. But oh my God, I like him now. That fast, I like Austere Man, because he's not really all that austere.

Of course, there's still that pesky girlfriend. *So stop it. Just be normal. You're fairly good at that most of the time.*

After I ring up his order, he passes me a credit card and I glance at the name. *Benjamin Page.* It's a nice name.

As I turn back to him with the card a few seconds later, I make a split-second decision. "You don't remember this, but we've met before."

I don't like dropping that on someone—it puts them on the spot—so as his eyes grow shaded with awkwardness, I rush ahead. I had enough awkwardness with him last time, after all. I only hope I don't create more of it now. "It was in Highland Cemetery, back in the spring. There was mud involved. And a very energetic Yorkie. I ended up with twigs in my hair. Ring any bells?"

His eyes go wide with recognition. And suddenly I'm wondering why on earth I took this pleasurable exchange and used it to implant in his brain the memory of me running hither and yon between tombstones, slipping and sliding on wet grass, trying to catch a runaway dog.

But I've done it, so I have to roll with it. Thus I keep going and ask, "How's Bella?"

He tilts his head, appearing surprisingly uncertain, and says, "I'm not sure."

"No?" I venture, confused.

"She was my girlfriend's dog, and we broke up."

"Oh. That's a shame," I say, pretty sure my eyes have gone wide as coffee mugs and that I don't look like I find it even remotely a shame.

He nods, glancing down. "Not really. Other than missing Bella, that is." He sounds sincerely sad about the dog, and I don't blame him—she was adorable. And now I'm *really* liking this guy. Which is just plain dangerous.

I hand him his card back, unsure what else to say. So I keep winging it. "I have to confess...I'm not sorry to run into you again. So you can see I'm not a total nut. And to apologize again about that day."

"I knew you weren't a nut," he says quietly. "I've been wishing I could apologize to you, too. It was sweet of you to chase Bella the way you did. And I wasn't very nice. I was having a bad day."

That's when an uncontrollable laugh escapes me. "*You* were having a bad day? Did you see me after all that?"

We share some laughter over the memory—whoa, who thought I'd ever laugh about *that*?—and Benjamin Page gives his head a speculative tilt to say, "I have to head to my meeting, but, uh...any chance you'd want to continue this conversation over dinner one night?"

My heart was already beating pretty fast, but now it goes wild, pounding so hard against my chest that I almost worry he'll see it through my sweater and apron. "That sounds nice," I say—and I smoothly grab up one of the bakery's business cards from a holder on the counter and scribble my personal number on back.

He takes it, and after a glance asks, "Um, what's your name?"

"Oh," I say, slightly embarrassed again. "Haley. Haley Munson."

"I'll text you, Haley Munson," he says with a grin as he starts taking backward steps toward the door.

I nibble my lip, tilt my head. "Sounds good." More instinctive flirtation. It's been awhile, but apparently it's like riding a bike. "Good luck with your meeting!" I call then. "I hope your donuts turn out celebratory!"

"Thanks! I'll let you know!"

The bell on the door tinkles as he walks out. After which I blow out a wildly happy breath I hadn't realized I was holding.

"Wow." It's Hannah, behind me, still 'wow'ing. I forgot she existed there for a few minutes.

I spin to look at her.

"Nicely done," she says. "I was sweating it a little when you reminded him about the cemetery, but it unfolded perfectly."

I start nodding, smiling. "It did, didn't it?"

When the door opens again, we both look up, instantly on guard in case something has brought him back–but instead, it's Aunt Nan. "How did it go? Did he remember you? Anything interesting happen?"

We both just gape at her.

I narrow my gaze and say, "Where on earth did you come from? Have you been spying on me?"

"Of course I have," she answers on a laugh.

And I begin to put the pieces together. "Wait a minute. Are you the woman who convinced him we had great coffee?"

"Guilty as charged. I recognized him on the street, so I dropped my bag to get his attention."

"Of course you did," I say, exchanging looks with my sister.

Aunt Nan is completely undaunted, of course. "I knew that if he was a gentleman and helped me with my purse that it was worth pursuing. If he didn't, I would have let him cross the street to Perk Me Up."

I flash a scolding look. "Surely you remembered he had a girlfriend."

She shrugs. "Sometimes things change."

And sometimes, much as I hate to admit it, she seems just a little bit magic to me. I admit, "It so happens that they did. They've broken up."

She looks hopeful. "And..."

"He asked me out."

"You're welcome," she says.

And part of me still wants to scold her. For forcing me up that hill almost six months ago and the disaster that ensued. For commandeering this guy on the street under false pretenses. For just general meddling.

But I'm too happy. Maybe I shouldn't be—maybe I should be cautious. I admittedly have a track record of getting all happy and giddy too soon and then comes heartbreak. But something about this feels...special. Like it started out too weird *not* to be special. And it's all thanks to her. So instead of scolding, I walk around the counter and give her a big hug.

4

Back to the Wedding Box

Haley

As Ben and I stare down at the beautiful gift, reflecting on how we met, he says,

"Okay, maybe you're right."

"I know I am. I mean, she's a wise woman in her way. Without her, I wouldn't have chased a dog for you on the day we met, and you wouldn't have chased a dog for me today. Without her, you never would have come into the bakery before your pitch meeting for the Talcrita Tower."

His gaze raises from the box in his hands to me. "What do you mean?"

I blink. "What do you mean what do I mean?"

"I came into the bakery because a lady literally dragged me down the street to—" His expression changes, jaw dropping. "Wait a minute. Are you telling me that woman was...?"

I feel my eyes widen with surprise. "I never told you that?"

He shakes his head.

"And you didn't recognize her when you met her later?"

Another head shake. "Weeks had passed. A lot had happened. I'd gotten the building deal, then fallen in love with you. It was a busy time."

"Well, *she* recognized *you* right away that day on the street. As soon as you left, she popped in and confessed that she'd seen you waiting for a Walk light and worked her magic."

He blows out a breath, clearly thinking back on the event and trying to wrap his head around this new information. "I can't believe I never put two and two together. But *of course* it was her. *Of course.*"

We share a laugh, and he adds, "Wow, I guess I owe her even more than I realized."

"Then the least we can do is not open the gift until...well, let's not even think about that," I tell him. "Let's just take it home and tuck it away in a closet. And who knows—maybe we'll *never* have a reason to open it."

And with the help of all those good memories, I try to put my brand new worries away along with the box.

5

Haley and Ben's One-Year Anniversary

Haley

Aunt Nan has always said love makes you blind. Not that love *is* blind, like the old adage—she means something else. She says that when you're in love, you feel so connected to the other person that it makes you forget you might not want all the exact same things or have the exact same taste, that it's easy to assume you see the world through the exact same lens.

So far, though, Ben and I haven't had that problem. It's not that we've never had a difference of opinion or hit a bump in the relationship road—early on, we both had our own insecurities to work through—but a year into our marriage, we're happy and well-suited.

And right now, we're walking hand-in-hand up the promenade at the Crestview Hills Town Center, looking for a one-year anniversary gift to ourselves. We decided it would be fun to go shopping together until we stumble upon something we both love. So far, we have a cute summer top for me, and a new pair of tennis shoes, also for me. I'm lucky he's a good sport. But we're working our way to a home décor shop, thinking we'll find something for the apartment that will be a reminder of our first year together.

These are examples of ways love has *not* made us blind. He knows I get easily distracted when shopping, and he's okay with that. And I know if I start spending too much too frivolously on shoes or purses, he'll gently remind me that we're not made of money and I'll reign myself in, because *I'm* okay with *that.* And when he made the suggestion that instead of trying to surprise each other with some impossibly perfect gift that we approach it another way, I was okay with that, too, since it kind of symbolized our ability to agree on things.

An ability which has kept Aunt Nan's wedding gift beautifully wrapped in its ivory paper and lace, residing on the top shelf of my closet. And though it occasionally comes to mind and I'm still dying to know what's inside, I'm starting to think we truly may never need to find out.

We spent our wedding night in a riverfront hotel room with a wide balcony providing a perfect view of the Cincinnati skyline—then jetted off to the Big Island for a truly dreamy honeymoon. Ben moved into my apartment—small, but in a cute historic building in the heart of Lakeside Park's business district. I can walk to work, it's only a mile from my parents' place, and its old-fashioned European façade gives it character. We're still saving to buy a house, but for now, it's the perfect little home for us. Ben's ten-minute commute across the bridge into the city for work has only turned into fifteen.

Ben stays busy, with Terence, managing architectural aspects of the Talcrita Tower as construction finally begins, while working on other projects for his firm as well. And while Hannah and I still spend our days creating and selling yummy treats, the Two Sisters Bakery has thrived enough that we now have a small staff, giving us most weekends off.

The home décor store is in sight—when a cute pair of sandals in a store window steals my attention. "So cute," I croon, inadvertently pulling Ben toward the window. Then I peek up at him. "I'm sorry—do you mind?"

He just laughs. "Would it matter?" But he's only teasing, and adds, "Take your time."

When we eventually reach the home shop, nothing really speaks to us, so we choose to move on. We're headed back to the car, giftless, when we pass by a large pet supply store hosting an animal adoption event. "Oh, look," I say.

And Ben quickly replies, "No, *don't* look. Put your pet blinders on."

He knows I'm a sucker for cute animals. And while we'd both like a pet, we agree the apartment is too small and we're committed to waiting until we have a bigger place. As I suspected, I see Puff a lot less these days, and catching sight of a few little cat faces tugs at my heart.

"You're right, you're right," I murmur, and as we walk past, I try to drown out the meows by doing the old, "La la la la la."

Ben

I'm sitting across from Haley at our favorite Italian restaurant, which happens to be next door to the bakery. We're celebrating our anniversary with dinner out and an evening back at the same hotel as on our wedding night.

Everyone here knows us, both due to the bakery's proximity and because we walk up for dinner at least once a week. Sometimes her parents join us, or Hannah and her husband, Dan—but more often than not, it's just the two of us. I never thought I'd be that guy—the one everybody knows by name when he walks in somewhere—but it's nice. One more thing Haley's given me—being part of a community.

"Dinner will be right up, you two," our waitress Robin says as she rushes past. DeGregorio's stays busy, but they always seem to find a table for us.

After our pasta dishes arrive, I raise my wineglass and look across the table to the girl I love. "To an amazing first year together. And all the years to come."

She blushes sweetly, and softly says, "I love you, Ben."

I reply, "I love you, too, babe," just before we dig in to the best spaghetti and meatballs in town.

As we eat, I say what's stayed on my mind all afternoon since our unsuccessful shopping trip. "I was thinking about our gift to ourselves, and I might have the perfect idea."

Her eyes widen hopefully. "Oh?"

"I know I told you to put your pet blinders on," I venture cautiously, "but...would it be so bad if we didn't wait? I wouldn't mind the pitter patter of little paws around the house, and I don't think you would, either. I know space is tight, but surely we can make room for one little furry guy—or girl."

She looks surprised at first, so I add, "I know, I know, we agreed it would make more sense later, so if you're not good with it—"

"No," she interrupts me, smiling. "You're right. It's kind of impulsive, which is usually more my vibe than yours, but... let's do it. It *is* the perfect gift to ourselves. A new little family member—one that isn't quite as dramatic as a baby."

We laugh at that—we're in *firm* agreement that babies should happen several years down the road and only when we have a *lot* more space. Yet this suddenly seems like a great decision, something we'll both be excited about. So much so that we both start talking quickly back and forth about it over our plates.

"I already can't wait," I tell her.

"Me, too!" She's all smiles across the table. "Finding our new little family member is going to be so fun."

Which is the perfect segue into the next part of my idea. "I want to show you something." I lower my fork and pick up my phone, murmuring, "I just need to find it."

As I'm looking, trying to locate the online post that caught my eye a few hours ago, I'm vaguely aware of her phone buzzing a notification. "Do you mind if I check this?" she asks.

Since I'm already looking at mine, I say, "Of course not."

When I've finally located the photo of five dogs, all beautiful shiba inus, rescued from a breeding mill and in need of homes, I say, "Okay, I've got it."

As I'm stretching my phone out for her to see, she looks

up from her own screen to say, "The most amazing thing just happened! Sienna texted me a picture of the cutest kitten in the world—and it needs a loving home! Or it's going to be taken to a shelter! It's like the universe heard what you just said and sent us this kitten!"

"Or...what about these dogs?" I suggest.

We're both holding out our phones across the table, but we're looking at each other instead. Her smile has faded into something more perplexed-looking, and I'm probably wearing a similar expression. "Take a look at them, babe," I tell her, trying to shift her attention to my phone. "It's a really sad story. They've been caged their whole lives, used for breeding."

"That's really horrible," she agrees. "But...I thought we'd get a cat. More specifically, a kitten. Like this one." She jiggles her phone at me. "My family got Puff when he was just a baby."

I lower my phone and start eating again, mainly to try to wrap my head around my confusion. A moment later, I look back up, squinting my doubt, to ask, "So you want a *cat*?"

She nods, and has *not* lowered *her* phone. "Of course I want a cat. You know I love cats."

Hmm. Okay, I guess I do know that, but... "Well, I love dogs. I thought we *both* loved dogs."

"I *like* dogs," she corrects me sternly. "But I *love* cats."

"Don't take this the wrong way," I begin, trying for a calm tone, "but why would we choose a cat over a dog?"

The look on her face tells me she did take it the wrong way and I haven't calmed anything at all. "Because cats take up way less space in an apartment? Because they take care of themselves and don't mind alone time when we're both working? Because they're cozy and curl up next to you when you read or watch TV?"

I blink, still thrown by this turn of events. So much that I can't even bring myself to admit she made some decent points. Because I just assumed. She knows I grew up with dogs; she knows I'm *great* with dogs. She knows I missed Bella after the Taryn breakup. And dogs are just so much more... "If you want a buddy, a dog is your buddy," I argue my point. "If you want love and companionship, look no further than a dog." I'm pointing my fork at her now as I say the words.

Her brow knits. "That's not what I said I wanted, so clearly you weren't even listening. And a dog, in our little apartment, sounds like a nightmare. Those particular dogs look *huge*."

"Huge?" I ask dubiously. "I'd call them more medium-size."

"Well, they're not small. And this kitten is tiny. Just like our apartment." More phone-jiggling on her part. "And it's the last of a litter. All her brothers and sisters have been given away—she's the only one left. And if she's taken to a shelter, who knows what fate awaits her? And look at those eyes!"

I try not to. The kitten has *enormous* eyes and I don't want to be drawn into the story Haley's creating around it. Instead I plead the case of the canines. "It so happens that shiba inus adapt well to small living spaces and don't mind spending time alone. They're loyal and affectionate, but gentle, too."

She takes all that in silently, appearing stubborn, which lets me know I've made some good arguments, as well.

So I put my fork back down and hold my phone back up. "And look how pretty they are. They look sort of like foxes."

Rather than look, though, she only says, "I just took for granted that when you said *pet, now*, you meant going about it in a sensible manner. As in picking one we won't trip over every five minutes."

I draw back slightly, affronted. We don't fight, Haley and I, ever, and her tone is jarring. "So you're calling me...the opposite of sensible? Reckless? Stupid? Something like that."

She blows out a breath—and though she'd just put her phone down to start eating again, now she lets her fork drop to her dish with a slight clatter. "I'm not calling you anything. Don't put words in my mouth."

"Well, maybe we should just forget the whole thing. If we can't agree on a pet, we just won't get one. And *none* of these animals will get homes." Aware I'm exaggerating, I lower my phone firmly to the table, then pick up my wineglass and toss back a swig, like it's a shot of whiskey.

"So you don't want to rescue a pet unless you get your way?"

"Well, if I don't get *my* way, then you get *your* way. And vice versa. So no matter what, one of us comes out the winner and one comes out the loser. Let's just forget it."

"Then *neither* of us gets what we want, and we don't help *any* animal in need. That's no solution."

Another fair point, but it also feels like manipulation. So I say, "It's the only answer that makes any sense to me." And I start eating again. More out of anger and the need to do something to distract me than an actual desire to eat. She, on the other hand, hangs her head, moping into her spaghetti.

She's making me feel like the big bad wolf, even though I've done nothing wrong. I ask, "Aren't you going to eat your dinner?"

"I've lost my appetite."

I sigh. Theatrics. "You know what doesn't help anything? Being overly-dramatic."

When her eyes go as wide as the plate in front of her, I know I've said the wrong thing. "Oh my God, did you really just call me a drama queen?"

"Um, no." Because I didn't say that at all. "But I think *you* just did."

She blows out a disgusted breath. "Well, maybe it's dramatic to me to realize how little you care about my feelings! You see how important this is to me, but you couldn't care less about making me happy."

I just blink, incredulous. "Aren't you doing the exact same thing? Acting like what I want doesn't matter at all?"

That stumps her and she stays quiet. But we're at an impasse. We've just acknowledged that we're not willing to put each other first.

"Well, happy anniversary to us," I grouse.

Just then, Robin comes rushing up with a large plate bearing a fancy-looking slice of cheesecake with a candle burning atop it, surrounded by chocolate cannolis. "Happy first anniversary!" she declares, placing the plate in the center of the table.

And before either of us can get our wits about us, here comes the whole waitstaff singing the very fast, very merry anniversary song once featured on *The Flintstones*. "Ohh-hhh...happy anniversary, happy anniversary!" I sit there, wide-eyed, dumbfounded, as the whole restaurant stares. I'm trying to smile, but I'm pretty sure it's not making it to my face. Haley looks to be in the same boat. We should be laughing, enjoying the funny song and the kindness being shown to us. I wish like hell I was handling it better. I flash back to the day we met and how much I regretted my bad behavior.

That, plus the fact that it's a pretty long song, eventually allows me to muster a smile. I even reach across the table toward my wife and hold out my hand.

She doesn't hesitate to take it. Which is reassuring. Our marriage isn't going to dissolve over this one argument.

When the singing finally ends, we join the whole restaurant in applause, and I manage a heartfelt, "Thank you—this is great! It looks awesome. I only hope we're not too full to eat it."

As the other waiters and waitresses drift off in different directions, Robin says, "I can always box it up for you." Then she winks. "Now I'll leave you guys to make an anniversary wish and blow out your candle."

As she walks away, our eyes meet again and I'm quick to say with a scolding grin what I know we're both thinking. "No wishing for a cat or a dog."

"You can't stop me from wishing," she retorts, both playful and defiant.

"Wish all you want," I tell her, "but I think we should table this for tonight." We've got a hotel room booked, after all. We don't have the luxury of going home and being mad at each other from separate rooms. We have to be romantic, damn it. "So here's my wish. I wish for us to have many more happy years together, and an awesome first anniversary tonight." I raise my eyebrows playfully.

It pulls a flirty smile from her. Then she focuses back on the candle burning between us. "My wish for us is...to agree on things we both care about."

"Good wish," I say. Even though I know she still wants a cat and I still want a dog.

An hour later, we're on the balcony of our hotel room, eating boxed cheesecake and taking in the view on a warm, clear June night. Some tension remains—neither of us have brought the argument back up, but it's lingering in the air. Not just the cat-or-dog question, but that we both assumed we wanted the same thing and then refused to budge.

When Haley sees me focusing on the skyline, though, she sets the to-go box down and comes to stand beside me. "Show me where the building will be again."

The Talcrita Tower is over there, under construction, just not visible yet from across the river because it's little more than a foundation so far. I point out where it'll stand in the skyline fairly often, but that changes depending on where we are when we're looking. "From here," I explain, "it's kind of behind the PNC Building and in front of the Carew Tower."

"I'm very proud of you," she tells me, still peering across the river, "for creating something that will be so...lasting."

I shift my focus from the city to her. "Thank you, babe," I answer, her words touching me unexpectedly. It's the kind of thing my grandpa would say if he were still here, so it's nice to hear from the person who's become my family.

"I'm proud of you, too," I inform her. I know she worked

hard to build the bakery with Hannah. "You took an empty storefront and made it a vibrant business."

She smiles her appreciation and jokes, "I guess we're just a couple of pillars of our community."

At which I turn to take her in my arms. "Well, this pillar is ready to have his way with the other pillar."

"And this pillar," she tells me, "couldn't be happier to hear that."

And suddenly, much as I love the skyline, I'm ready to trade in the view for something even better.

6

Haley

Two days after our anniversary I'm hanging out in the bakery with Hannah, our mom, Aunt Nan, and Sienna. We're closed, having a private tasting of some new wedding cake flavors Hannah has concocted.

"Final votes?" Hannah asks. We've done all the eating and some discussing already.

"The banana cream rocks," Sienna says. "And I loved the salted caramel. But the lemon was a little tart for me."

Hannah nods. "Mom? Aunt Nan?"

Mom says, "Well, you know I'm partial to red velvet, so that's a win for me. And I agree on the banana cream—very yummy. The caramel didn't set my soul on fire. And I agree with Sienna on the lemon—too tart."

Aunt Nan is nodding already. "Yes, the lemon is too... lemony."

"Okay, got it, back to the drawing board on the lemon,"

Hannah says just a bit briskly. It's never fun to get a crummy review, even when the rest of your art is well received.

"But the decadent chocolate?" Aunt Nan imitates a French chef blowing a kiss. "*Tres' magnifique.*"

My sister smiles, her emotions clearly soothed.

"*You're* uncharacteristically quiet," she says then, casting a suspicious look my way. I guess I'm a little withdrawn and she's just now noticing.

"Oh," I say, distracted. "I liked the banana, too. Really, I liked everything but the—"

"Lemon," she interrupts me. "Got it."

"Well, you asked."

"How was your anniversary celebration?" Aunt Nan cuts in on our squabble to inquire. One of her simple wise ways: See someone nattering uselessly—change the subject to something better. Or at least she *thought* this was a better subject.

"Yes, I forgot to ask," Mom chimes in. "Was it an oh-so-romantic evening?" She raises her eyebrows suggestively.

Normally, I would laugh and play along, but instead I just answer, "It was fine."

And they all exchange puzzled looks. Usually a question like that would have me waxing poetic about every aspect of the evening.

"Now that I think about it," Hannah says, "you've been weird and quiet all day. What's up?"

"Well, during dinner," I begin slowly, "we had a big fight."

Their collective gasp validates my horror. They know we don't fight.

"Whatever about?" Mom asks.

"Whether cats or dogs are better pets."

More puzzled looks flit between them all. Finally, it's Sienna who attempts to express their group confusion with squinty eyes and a sound like "Whaaa...?"

"We decided to get a pet," I explain, "even though we always thought we'd wait until we moved. But then he showed me these big dogs who are were rescued from some breeding place, assuming I'd consider it the perfect pet. And I feel for the dogs, of course, but right then Sienna texted me about a kitten in need of adoption." I glance at her. "She didn't even know we were thinking of getting a pet, so the timing seemed heaven-sent, and I fell in love with the picture and can already practically feel her in my arms. And after that, well..." I shrug hopelessly. "It just devolved. Into the merits of cats versus dogs. And why we each wanted our way."

I don't meet anyone's eyes for fear of seeing they find this a pretty silly fight.

"How did it end?" Sienna asks.

"The entire staff of the restaurant appeared out of nowhere singing us an anniversary song, so we set it aside. And neither of us have brought up since."

I let out a sigh and go on. "But it's still on my mind. And I'm not sure I can stay quiet much longer. Keeping the peace is nice, but not talking about the problem won't make it go away. And sure, we *could* just let this go away—it's not life or death that we have a pet—but it seems like a bad precedent to set, just ignoring the thing we can't agree on. It's become the elephant in the room."

"Maybe that's the answer—get an elephant," Mom cheerfully suggests.

When I shoot her a look, she gets more serious and says, "What I mean is—maybe you should just get some entirely different animal so that no one is disappointed. A nice bird perhaps."

"I don't want a bird," I snap.

"A turtle?" Sienna offers. "I had a turtle when I was a kid and I loved it."

I feel like they're missing the point, so I restate it. "We thought we knew each other so well, but apparently we don't. And we also don't seem to care much about making each other happy." A notion which makes me sulk over my cake plate.

"If you want to know what *I* think," Aunt Nan says, "it's that it should have been obvious to both of you that he'd want a dog and you'd want a cat. *I* knew that. If you'd have asked me, I'd have told you. But it's like I always say—love makes you blind."

Oh. Wow. It does suddenly make a sad sort of sense now—I've been so in love with Ben that I've just assumed he feels the same as me about *everything*. It's like I thought we share the same brain or something. Which is silly. I'd really started to believe we'd never disagree about *anything*. Which, now that I think about it, seems pretty preposterous.

"Well, what do we do about it?" I ask my wise aunt. "And please don't say get a bird or a turtle."

"What you do," she says, reaching out to cheerfully pat my hand, "is have a little faith. You go meet the dogs. You go meet the kitten. You both go into it with an open heart, knowing that the right pet will find you. *We* don't really find *them*, you know—*they* find *us*. You'll both know when you fall in love with the right one, and you'll naturally agree. It's that simple."

I don't think it's that simple at all, but I don't say so.

After I lock up the bakery and we all say goodnight, I pout my way up the sidewalk toward home.

When I walk in, Ben is sitting at the kitchen table. "Hey," he says. But his voice lacks its usual warmth.

"Hi." Mine does, too.

"How was the big wedding cake tasting?" He's trying—I can tell—but there's still that stupid elephant standing metaphorically between us.

"Banana cream won the day."

"That sounds awful to me," he confesses with an endearing smile.

And my heart softens a little. Just like when he took my hand at the restaurant the other night, I'm reminded that we love each other. "You'd probably be in Aunt Nan's camp on the decadent chocolate."

"Sounds delicious," he says.

"I should have brought some home to you."

"Even though you're still mad at me?"

I hold up a bakery bag, telling him, "Be that as it may, I did bring you this." Without looking, he knows it's a jelly donut. Neither a celebratory nor conciliatory one—more of a comforting one. It's true that a donut is good for any occasion.

He makes a slight gesture toward the kitchen counter behind him, where a single daisy now resides in a bud vase.

More reminders that we love each other. I sigh, then set

my things down and lean over to give him a hug.

After which he pushes to his feet, then reaches out to take my hand. "Listen, why don't we try to talk about it without being mad, okay?"

Together we walk to the sofa and sit down. We stay quiet a minute until I gently ask, "It's really that important for you to have one of those dogs?"

"Maybe it sounds childish, but...dogs are really the only animals I've ever felt a connection to. Given the way my childhood went, I've probably felt close to more dogs than I have people. I feel like we can give a dog who's had a challenging life a good home, and I think that would be meaningful to us both. And to tell you the truth, I don't even like cats."

I gasp.

And he adds, "I don't *dislike* them—I just don't feel any particular affinity for them."

I blow out a heavy breath, stunned and a little wounded. "But I *love* cats. I mean, I adore them! You know how I feel about Puff. And pretty much *any* cat I see *anywhere*."

He looks a little guilty then. "I guess I do, but I...just never thought about it. You love *lots* of things. I guess I thought cats were just among the millions of things that draw your attention—like boots or dresses or daisies or snowmen or a good Christmas lights display."

"Okay, fair enough," I admit. I do ooh and ahh over a lot of things. "But cats are different for me."

"Believe me, I'm getting that now."

"And you...can't even be *open* to a cat?"

He blinks uncertainly. I can tell he's just trying to find

the most diplomatic way to say no. "Maybe...eventually. But I know dogs, Haley." He keeps saying that. And I suspect there's more to it, words he can't find because he's a guy's guy. But these particular words aren't cutting it with me.

"Well, you can come to know cats, too," I try to persuade him.

He presses his lips tight together, then releases a sigh. "And you really couldn't be open to a shiba inu?"

"Look around us." I demonstrate, doing just that. "This place is too small for a dog, even a little one. I would consider a dog in a few years, but a kitten makes so much more sense for where we are right now. And it would make me so happy." I smile, trying to remind him he *loves* making me happy—happy wife, happy life and all that.

But instead he only replies, "In the same way coming home to a dog greeting me at the door would make *me* happy."

"Which is fair," I confess. "I understand that now. I do care about your happiness. But turns out we both want different qualities in our pet."

"I care about your happiness, too, babe," he tells me. "I hate that you think I don't."

I shake my head. "No, I know you do. It just...appears we can't agree on this particular issue."

He nods. Then slowly lifts his gaze to mine. "Are you thinking what I'm thinking?"

"That it's time to open the box?" I gingerly ask. "Aunt Nan's gift?"

"Yep."

It's funny, we don't talk about the wedding box—I'm not

sure if we've talked about it since we put it in the closet—but I guess it's lingered in the back of both our minds, as we knew it would. Only...it's *worried* me less the longer we've gone without having to open it. It *wasn't* some dark harbinger of misery after all—our marriage wasn't doomed by it.

So I don't hesitate to push to my feet, walk to my bedroom closet, pull down a hat box where I keep hair accessories, then retrieve the beautifully-wrapped gift from behind it. The bow remains perfectly in place, the ivory silk roses, too. I carry it back to the living room and set it between us on the couch.

"Ready?" I say, reaching for the ribbon.

"Sure," he says. "We'll finally get to see what's in here."

For some reason I hesitate—maybe because it's so pretty and I'm about to destroy that—but as I begin to pull gently at the ribbon, Ben says, "Wait. Are we sure we want to do this?"

I release it and look up. "She said to open it when we had our first big disagreement."

He sighs, appearing dejected and resigned. "You're right. Go ahead."

Only...I don't. Instead I say, "But it's also true that we only get to open this once. After we open it, we don't have it to fall back on anymore. So are we one-hundred percent sure this is what we want to use it on?"

Instead of answering the question, though, he tilts his head and says, "You know, one thing that bothers me about this is that we were both so surprised by it. I thought we knew each other so well."

"Me, too," I agree, giving him a sad smile. "But it's like Aunt Nan says—love makes you blind."

7
Before...

Haley

Ben and I have been texting and talking on the phone for a week and we're finally going out tonight. He's been crazy busy with work since he came into the bakery—because the people he was meeting with hired his company on the spot. This is the first project he and his best friend have spearheaded, so it's a big deal.

I snap a picture of a wedding cake Hannah and I have just put the finishing touches on—with fresh daisies on top and strategically placed in a few spots on each tier. I text the pic to Ben for fun.

He texts back: *You're talented.* And then: *More daisies, I see.*

I have no idea what he's talking about, so I type: *???*

He answers: *When I met you in the cemetery, you were wearing a top with daisies on it.*

Wow. I can't believe he remembers that. My heart warms

because it means he was paying more attention than it seemed like. But I answer matter-of-factly: *Daisies are my favorite flower. Just a coincidence that the bride who ordered this wedding cake likes them, too. That poor T-shirt will never be the same, though.*

He replies: *No?*

I answer: *Grass stains.*

In response I get a frowny face. Which really sums it up completely. And, though ironic perhaps, makes me smile.

Hours later, I'm in front of the full-length mirror in my bedroom, trying to look pretty for our date. Cute sundress—check. Hair down, looking bouncy and pretty—check. Butterflies in stomach and heart beating a mile a minute—also check, and even though those last two weren't part of the plan, I tell myself it's better to be nervous and excited than calm and indifferent. And, well, okay, I'm a little on guard, too. I don't want to get hurt again. So it's kind of scary to let myself be so happy and optimistic. But I remind myself that he, for some reason, already has Aunt Nan's seal of approval—and that seems important.

My windows are open on this first day that's felt like summer giving way to fall. Outside, leaves rustle in a gentle breeze and it seems like a perfect evening for romance. When the doorbell rings, my heart skitters, but I take a deep breath, smooth my dress, and go answer.

On the other side stands a handsome man in jeans and a button-down, holding a bouquet of daisies. As my gaze drops to the flowers, he asks, "Too clichéd?"

"Not at all. I love them." *I love* you. Well, that's an insane and overreactive thought—thank God I didn't say it. Maybe I just meant I *love that you're the kind of guy who pays attention and wants to impress me.*

I take them, aware of our hands touching during the exchange—a connection moves all through me. "Let me put them in water before we go," I say with a smile.

He steps in to my apartment, only slightly bigger than a studio with one main living space plus a bedroom and bath, so he's standing in the kitchen and living room at the same time. "Cute place."

"It's little, but I like it."

In my peripheral vision I notice him glancing around, taking in details. I suppose architects see spaces from a different perspective. "The building feels unique—and I like the façade. Bavarian Tudor...with a hint of Deco I wouldn't have expected."

"I never thought about it being Deco," I reply with a tilt of my head, "but you have a good eye since it was built in 1929. Back then, this whole building was only four apartments—but somewhere along the way it was divided into twenty. Fortunately, I don't need much space, and I like the history of it, and the walkability of the neighborhood."

He peeks out a window, looking up and down the street. "I haven't spent much time in this neighborhood," he says. "I like it, though. It's got that quaint, laidback thing going for it."

I point in the general direction of the bakery and surrounding establishments. "There's a drugstore around the corner, and it's pretty easy to grab dinner or a drink."

"Or a jelly donut." He grins. "Maybe I should *start* spending some time here."

He's a bit of a flirt. My smile and the playfully shy dip of my chin flirts back. "Maybe so."

"Ready?" he asks.

I nod, grabbing the sweater I laid out.

"I hope it didn't seem odd, me wanting to pick you up," he says. "I know it's not the usual way on a first date these days."

I didn't think it was strange when he suggested it, even though maybe I should have. Ax murderers and all. Have all those true-crime documentaries taught me nothing? And I know it's totally naïve to be sure he's not one. But I'm still pretty sure, so I reply, "I thought it seemed gentlemanly."

"I guess that's what I was going for." Though he appears almost unhappy with himself as he adds, "I'm not usually so old-fashioned."

I raise my eyebrows. "What's the occasion?"

He considers the question before replying, "Well, my grandpa always told me that when you meet a girl you really like, you pick her up, take her flowers, and walk her to the door at the end of the evening."

I smile at his candor. Or maybe it's more flirtation. Or both. If it's just a line, it's a pretty good one. "I think I'd like your grandpa."

8

He takes me to a trendy eatery in a historic building near the Roebling Suspension Bridge, where we get a table in the back courtyard, an area with lots of old brick and greenery.

A bottle of wine accompanies dinner, a meal filled with smiles, getting-to-know-you talk, and a growing sense of ease. He asks about the bakery and I explain how the very act of baking makes me feel like I'm putting something sweet into the world and that's why it's satisfying to me every single day. The weird thing is, I never knew that before. Not until I heard the words come out of my mouth with Ben.

He tells me he can relate since that's kind of why he became an architect. "To add something to the world," he says. I learn he graduated from UC before he and his best friend got internships at the same downtown firm until both were hired on permanently.

When I ask about this big building he and his friend just designed, I hear the excitement in his voice. "The thing I'm most looking forward to is watching it go up, looking out on the skyline and knowing that particular part of it is there because of me."

After dinner, we take a walk to Riverside Drive, a historic street lined with pre-Civil War mansions on one side and the Ohio River on the other, with the best view of the Cincinnati skyline in town. Across the wide Ohio, the Reds are playing, so the baseball stadium is lit up, along with the rest of the city —lights twinkle in countless rows of windows, and the curves and lines of the suspension bridge are illuminated by the last vestiges of the sunset. As we stroll along, Ben points out where his building will be among the dozens already there, and even after that, I notice how frequently his eye seems drawn to the cityscape.

I, however, tend to notice the grand old houses on the opposite side of us more, each unique unto itself. "When I was little," I tell him, "I used to fantasize about living in one of these houses someday."

He glances over at them and agrees, "They're pretty awesome. And this view." Then he points away from the river. "I live about ten blocks in that direction. After college I moved into an old house split into apartments, and my grandpa lived there with me before he died."

"Really?" He's mentioned his grandpa before, but no one else in his family. I sense a story there, one that might tell me a lot more about this smooth, handsome man I'm growing more smitten with by the moment. "Was this the same grandpa who taught you to be gentlemanly with a date?"

He nods easily. "Yep."

I bite my lip in hesitation, worried I'm prying too soon,

being my ever-nosy self, but then I ask him what I want to know. "Is it his grave you were visiting that day in the cemetery?"

Another nod. "Also yes."

I glanced at the headstone after he left that first day. And many times after. I keep that part to myself, but I can see it clearly in my mind. *Edward C. Page. Beloved husband, father, and grandfather.*

"How is it that he came to live with you?" I ask.

And now he's the one hesitating.

I feel pushy, like I ruined the easy vibe between us. But I don't think it's an odd question since he mentioned it.

Finally, he glances over and says, "That's a long story."

That's it. His whole answer. We keep walking. I feel awkward. But before I can stop it, I hear myself say, "I'm not in a hurry. If you want to tell me."

He doesn't respond right away. And the trouble with me, Sienna claims, is that I'm such a talker, such an open book, that I don't respect that not everyone is. Yet it's not that I don't respect it, it's that I...just don't understand it. If I like someone, I'm okay letting them know who I am—the good, the bad, and the ugly.

Finally, not looking at me, he says, "It's pretty heavy for a first date." Which kind of knocks the wind out of my sails. Because it's not just a long story—now it's a *heavy,* long story. And that open-bookness in me always expects the other person to just get okay with it and want to give me their entire life history.

I should take the hint, though. I should totally take the hint and shut up and talk about something else.

But at the same time I still want to know everything about him. And when you feel that way, nothing is too heavy. So I promise, "I can take it if *you* can." After which I tease him a little. "And you can't really put something like that out there without telling me."

When he doesn't reply, though, I realize I might be messing this up. So I rush into an awkward apology. "I'm sorry—I don't mean to pry. My friends tell me I'm too nosy, and I don't always catch myself until I've already nosed." I'm tilting my head, smiling as I self-deprecate, trying to be light. "And you actually *can* put that out there without telling me. So let's talk about something else. Binged any good TV shows lately? What kind of music do you like?"

I've made him laugh now, which is good. Except I still feel like what I am—a nosy, pushy girl. And the date will probably go south from here, and I'll never see him again and have only a vase of soon-to-be-dead daisies and a grass-stained T-shirt to remember him by.

"No," he says, smiling, about the binging. "And a lot of different kinds—from bluegrass to rock."

I nod, with no idea where to direct the conversation now as he motions to a park bench facing the city. After we take a seat, he tells me, "The thing is, my parents died when I was ten."

Whoa. I'm glad we're sitting. I start blinking nervously because he's just said something so shocking, so unexpected, and I kind of made him do it. He warned me it was heavy, but I guess I was too intoxicated by him to prepare myself for something so intense. "I'm so sorry," I murmur. But I'm sure a million people have said that, so it feels empty.

He glances at me only briefly, clearly uncomfortable with the topic. "They were killed in a car accident. After that, I went to live with my grandpa, my dad's dad. He raised me."

I'm stunned and want to ask more, but that would definitely be a bridge too far—I've already pushed him to tell me something he didn't want to, and if he cared to say anything else about it, he would be saying it. So I take what I hope is a safer road, for both of us. "What was that like, living with your grandpa?"

As he considers his answer, I think he's relieved I took that road, too, and maybe didn't expect it because I clearly have no respect for personal boundaries. Sienna is so right about me. His tone holds less weight as he shrugs and says, "It was nice, actually." Then he laughs. "I didn't always think so —he lived on a farm and ran a dog kennel out of a barn on the ridge behind the house, so it was a lot of work—but all in all, it was as good a childhood as I could have asked for under the circumstances."

This warms my heart—which has spent the last thirty seconds or so breaking for his loss. "So you and he got along well together," I say.

"Yeah, we were close. Always. But especially after I went to live with him. My grandma had died a few years before, and I was an only child, so I guess we...appreciated each other, you know?"

I think of my own family—not just Mom and Dad and Hannah, but Aunt Nan and other aunts and uncles, grandparents, Hannah's husband and kids—and I feel unduly blessed, like I've taken them all for granted. "I'm glad you had each other," I say. Then immediately fear it came out sounding maudlin. So I revert to something safe again. "What was it like to live on a farm? And where is it? Do you still have it?"

His grin tells me my naïve suburban roots are showing.

I laugh and confess, "Yes, I'm one of those people who get a little excited when I see a cow."

"And you moo at it," he says.

I draw back slightly, dumbstruck. "How did you know?"

His eyebrows lift knowingly. "*Everybody* from the city moos when they see a cow in a field. Seriously. Every friend I ever took home from college felt the need to moo at the cows."

"I had no idea." I tilt my head, thinking back on occasional excursions to the country. It somehow seemed natural and fun to let out a moo. "Well," I promise, "if you show me your cows, I will resist the urge."

His laugh makes things feel nice again, less dark and heavy. "We sold the farm years ago," he says. And I'm kind of disappointed, but on the other hand, slightly relieved I'll never be expected to milk a cow or feed a chicken if I were to become his girlfriend. "It was about two hours south of here."

"Tell me more about it," I request, still interested. I never would have pegged him for a farm boy. From his car to his suit to, well, his entire demeanor, he had city slicker written all over him that first odd time we met.

"We raised a few head of cattle," he began, "and about twenty chickens, for eggs, and we had a small garden—corn, potatoes, green beans, that sort of thing—but life was mostly about the kennel. Because it was pretty much twenty-four-seven. Things slacked up some in winter, but it was a year-round job. Big dogs, small dogs—I got to work with about every breed there is. When I got home from school, my first job was to feed and run the dogs."

"Run them?"

"Let them out of their pens into a fenced corral behind the barn where they could exercise and play. Even on rainy days, or cold ones, we got them out if they wanted to be. We tried to keep them happy when their families were away and they already felt scared and abandoned."

"That sounds difficult," I say. "To have to deal with sad, frightened dogs all the time. That would make *me* sad, too."

He slants me a soft grin. "You get used to it. And you learn how to calm them down and show them enough affection to get them through the week or so they're stuck with you." He laughs softly. "I actually loved it. I didn't know it at the time, but I did."

I find myself thinking it wouldn't be a job for a hard man, a man without love to give. And I remember how sweet he was with Bella the Yorkie when I so clumsily chased her back into his arms. An unexpected warmth spreads through my chest and down into my stomach.

"How come you sold the farm?" Crap. He told me his grandfather died, and that's probably why, and now I've stumbled back into the heavy, awkward stuff again.

"Well, it was a big deal for me to go to college," he confides. "No one in my family ever had. And I got some scholarships, so that helped. But it still left a lot of debt, as it does for most people. So one weekend my senior year when I went home, Grandpa Ed said to me, 'Ben, I been thinkin'. Way I see it is—me and you are kind of a team at this point.'

And he went on to say that he'd never wanted to tell me, but ever since I went away to school he'd been lonely. And running the farm and kennel were getting to be too much for him. So he proposed that he sell the farm, give me the money I needed to pay off my loans, and that we get a place together."

"Wow," I say, surprised to learn I was wrong about the reason for selling. "That was generous."

"That's what I said, too," Ben replies, "but he pointed out that whenever he died, the farm would be mine anyway. And he thought it made more sense to pay off my loans early *and* allow him to retire. When he put it like that, I had to agree."

"Was it hard to let the place go?"

He looks wistful. "Things like that always are. But it was a smart decision." Then he smiles. "And he liked the change. He'd lived here in the city as a young man—just like me, he'd left the farm and headed north. He learned brick masonry and made a good living at it. Only then he met a country girl, my grandma, who lured him back to the hills."

When he pauses, I venture, "Do you think anything will ever lure *you* back?"

His answer comes with a quick, firm head shake. "No. And Grandpa knew that, too—he knew I loved he city and wasn't ever coming home. That was part of his plan—I didn't have to give up anything I loved to have him near."

"And you liked living with him again, even as an adult?"

He smiles. "You'd think maybe sharing the same roof with my grandfather would cramp my style, but it didn't. He wasn't the type to keep tabs on me, and it worked out well for us both. It's not even a great neighborhood—a real mixed bag kind of place with hipsters trying to make it cool, old folks who've been there forever, sketchier people there because it's still low-rent. But Gramps liked that about it—he called it a crossroads of culture. And it was cool to see him re-embrace a lifestyle he'd given up so long ago. The place has been kind of lonely ever since he died, though, and I'm probably ready to move on. I just haven't gotten around to looking for anyplace better yet."

I swallow uncomfortably then because the next question is obvious—only I don't want him to look back on this night as a major downer. But I ask anyway, because there's no getting around it. "How did he die?"

"The man was healthy as a horse," Ben says, "until he suddenly wasn't. He got an infection and became septic. It happened fast—over just a couple of weeks. Really terrible weeks, but at least it wasn't long and drawn out."

Yep, more heaviness. And I feel sad that I'll never meet this man who was so important to him. "I'm sorry," I whisper. It sounds empty, but it's from the heart.

"The good thing," he tells me, looking more upbeat again, "is that he got to spend the last few years of his life taking it easy, no longer working day in and day out, and he got to spend them with me. We went to Reds games and Bengals games, and to my surprise, he even liked taking in some of the local museums. So if he had to go when he did...well, we had some good times before it happened."

As if on cue, the roar of the crowd erupts from the ballpark across the river and booming fireworks light up the sky. "Home run," we both say at the same time, then share a smile. We stop chatting to enjoy the moment.

After which he says, "You're easy to talk to."

This throws me. I mean, I am—everyone I know thinks so —but I wasn't sure *he* would, given my nosiness. "Thanks," I say, biting my lower lip modestly. Maybe even flirtatiously. Could be I haven't blown this to smithereens after all.

"I don't usually...talk that much," he admits. "About my past. Real things."

"I'm sorry if I made you do it against your will."

"I could have shut up if I wanted to. Like I said, you're nice to talk to."

My skin tingles just from the way he's looking at me. "You, too," I say softly. And even if it took some prodding, I'm touched that he chose to share something personal with me. Though I'm a little stuck on finding out his parents died so tragically when he was only a little boy.

Just then, a fluffy black cat comes trotting up the brick sidewalk, drawing my eye. "What a gorgeous cat," I coo. I'm drawn to *any* cat, but this one's a stunner. As it approaches, spotting us on the bench it's about to pass, it hesitates, so I bend slightly and offer a soft, "Here, kitty."

Slowly, the cat ventures forward, and I hold my hand down. There's still hesitation, though, so I promise in a whisper, "It's all right. You can trust me."

Soon the cat sniffs at my hand, then looks up at me and meows. Probably thought I had food and is let down. But I like that it's visiting with us. "Hello there, pretty kitty."

I want to pet it, but sometimes the move frightens a cat who doesn't know you, so I ever-so-gently ease my fingertips under its chin to gently touch. The cat flinches, but doesn't bolt, instead cautiously letting me stroke the smooth fur beneath its mouth. When it lifts its head to give me better access, I know we've become friends.

Even so, I'm delightfully surprised when the cat bounds up on the bench between Ben and me in that gentle cat way, eager to rub its head against my hand. "Oh my goodness, aren't you a sweetie," I say to the cat, smiling as Ben and I exchange amused looks.

As I proceed to pet the cat, beginning to wonder where it belongs—it has a collar, but no tag—a middle-aged woman rushes up the sidewalk toward us. "Sorscha, is that you?" Then she presses a palm to her chest in relief. "Thank goodness—it is." To me she adds, "Don't let her jump down or I'll never catch her."

To me, this cat does not seem hard to catch, but some can be docile one moment and on-the-run the next. So while continuing to pet the pretty kitty with one hand, I use the other to hook my index finger around her collar. "I've got her," I say.

The woman nods, still appearing relieved. Riverside Drive is relatively quiet, but the surrounding area is urban with high traffic and a million nooks and crannies a runaway cat could disappear into. "I opened the door to bring in a package and out she ran."

"I'm so glad you found her."

"Or you did," the woman replies. "She can be skittish—she must like you."

"I like her, too," I say, scooping the cat into my arms to hand her off. "Back to your mommy now, Sorscha. But it was very nice to meet you. Thank you for letting me pet you."

A moment later, Sorscha and her mom are heading back

in the direction they came, and Ben says admiringly, "You must be the cat whisperer."

I cast him a smug sideways glance. "I do have a way with cats."

He tilts his head, looking entertained. "Tell me more."

"I'm very fond of all cats," I explain. "And if I see a cat, I'm going to try to befriend it, so just know that about me going in—I will slow down any excursion or outing if a cat comes onto the scene."

He laughs, asking, "Do you *have* a cat? I didn't see any signs of a pet at your place."

"My cat lives at my parents' house," I explain. "Puff was raised there and it seemed unwise to take him with me when I got my own place. Of course, my mother thinks he's *our* cat, the whole family's, but he's really mine. My buddy. He used to sleep with me every night."

"Lucky cat," he says.

And heat climbs my cheeks as we exchange flirtatious looks.

Just then, cheers and a lot more fireworks explode across the river, illuminating the sky and sending trails of light reflecting across the water below. "Looks like a win," Ben says softly.

"Yep, looks like," I reply.

When his gaze drops to my lips, lingering there only briefly before he leans in to kiss me, I win, too.

9

Back to the Wedding Box

Ben

Sitting with the gift between us on the couch, so close to finally being opened, we've instead stopped to reminisce about our first date. We concede to each other how clear it was that I'm a dog person and she's a cat person, and that we're both idiots for not grasping the obvious.

"I guess we somehow missed that about each other," she says sadly. "I'm sorry."

I reach out, take her hand. "I'm sorry, too, babe." Then I smile wistfully, thinking back to that time, which was about a lot more than cats and dogs. Maybe that's why we failed to retain those parts. "It was a great night, though, wasn't it?"

She nods, squeezing my hand. "Maybe if love makes us blind, at least it means we're head over heels in it. Maybe it's a weird perk to love you so much that I assume you see the world through my eyes."

Falling a little more in love with her in this very moment, I glance down at the box, the thing literally separating us right now, to say, "We're not really gonna open this today, are we?"

She answers by telling me, "Aunt Nan said we should go meet the kitten and the shiba inus and just have faith that the right pet will find us. That we'll both know and agree, and it won't matter so much whether it's a cat or a dog—it'll just be the right one."

Hmm. It's a nice idea, but I'm pretty sure we'll end up right back where we started. Or maybe I'm wrong. "Maybe we should," I reply. I *hope* Aunt Nan is right and I'm wrong.

Haley gives a that-settles-it nod and says, "Let's just put the box back for now."

10

Haley and Ben's Two-Year Anniversary

Haley

Aunt Nan always says home is more of an idea than a place, and that the idea can be ever-changing. As is sometimes the case with Aunt Nan, it sounds full of wisdom, but I'm not really sure what it means. All I know is that *our* home, the one I've shared with Ben for two years now, has grown stressful.

I'm seeking a few minutes of morning peace on the couch with a cup of coffee when I hear the yowl of a cat whose tail just got stepped on. The cat darts from the bedroom, looking like she's been tortured, as Ben lets out a, "Geez, Emma, sorry —but for crying out loud, you're right under my feet when I'm trying to put my pants on."

Next thing I know, the cat has startled the dog, who then gallops across the room toward me, in a fright. I make the mistake of setting my mug down on a coaster—just in time for the dog's massive, fox-like tail to sweep the cup off the coffee table, coffee splattering everywhere. I cry out and Ben comes running—pants unzipped, a not-yet-buttoned white shirt hanging open over a T-shirt to say, "What the...?"

I'm standing there, arms outstretched, taking in the mess, and he just shakes his head.

"Daphne," I say, diverting my attention to the dog, "you are a walking disaster sometimes."

"Are you burnt?" Ben asked.

I shake my head. "No, it was only lukewarm. I'm more worried about the carpet."

We both fly into action—I'm grabbing paper towels from the kitchen and he's fetching real towels from the bathroom. I trip over the cat and nearly break my neck coming back. Ben, meanwhile, apparently forgets about the beautiful drafting table my parents got him for Christmas but which has no business in a tiny apartment already packed to the gills and bangs his hip into the edge as he re-enters the living room. "Damn it!"

"Geez, are you okay?"

He shakes it off. "Eh, what's one more bruise from the obstacle course we call home?"

As we sop up the spilled coffee, I spy Daphne cowering in the corner from all the yelling. She's a shy, easily-frightened but incredibly sweet dog, one of the five rescued shiba inus Ben saw online last summer. She indeed looks like a golden fox and came already named in a way that stuck, so whereas I named Emma after my favorite Jane Austen character, our dog bears the name of Scooby Doo's female sleuth friend. I like the name and Ben has learned to live with it.

After the sopping, I comfort the dog. "It's okay, nothing's

wrong. You're still a good girl," I tell her, running my fingers through her thick fur.

Ben joins me, kneeling down to nuzzle her and whisper soothingly in her ear. "Calm down, little girl, you're okay. We're all okay." He really does have a way with dogs—her trembling lessens at the very sound of his voice.

Never one to be left out of anything, Emma comes trotting up, so we include her in the love fest. Though she's a full-grown cat now, as a kitten she stole both our hearts with her big ears and big, needy eyes, just as I knew she would. Our brown and white kitty still possesses both, and she and Daphne are besties.

Normally, I'd already be at the bakery, but I have a dental appointment. So much for thinking I'd get a nice, quiet morning. I tell Ben, "Go ahead and get ready so you won't be late—I'll handle the rest of the cleanup."

He leans over, kisses me quickly, and says, "You're the best," before heading back to the bedroom—just narrowly missing the corner of the drafting table this time.

A few minutes later, he's out the door, briefcase in hand, and though I'd like to say peace is restored, I actually have a mewling cat at my feet, letting me know her breakfast is late and she's not going to stand for it. "Relax," I tell her. "It's coming." She amuses herself by batting at the undone tie on my robe as I wrangle some Meow Mix into a bowl with some milk: cat cereal.

Of course, the answer to our pet dilemma turned out to be simple—and complicated. We both fell in love with Emma, and then we both fell in love with Daphne, and when we realized we were already emotionally committed to both, Ben laughed and said, "Instant family!" We convinced ourselves it would just make the apartment all the more cozy.

And boy, does it ever. Whenever we're busy tripping over animals, we remind each other we both wanted the pitter patter of little paws—and we sure have plenty now! And we laugh it off, but on this particular morning Aunt Nan's words are ringing especially hollow to me. Home might be more of an idea than a place, but this place has gotten too cramped.

Ben

Haley's parents hosted a great family dinner celebrating our second anniversary, and now we're in the car, heading back to our wedding night hotel, same as last year, for a *private* celebration. The good news is that this year we're not in a fight about anything. The odd part, though, is... "Is it weird of me," I ask as we near the hotel, "that I'm excited about a night in a big, spacious room where we won't be tripping over anything?"

She flashes a slightly self-deprecating look. "I feel exactly the same way."

Twenty minutes later, when we should be getting romantic in our beautiful room, instead we're both walking around it, spreading our arms wide, talking about how great it is having nothing—or no one—underfoot.

A few minutes later, as we step out onto the balcony, wineglasses in hand, to take in the skyline, Haley remarks, "It's so big!" She means the balcony, not the city.

I draw my gaze from the view to my wife, giving her a smile. Ours at home is tiny. And yeah, "small balcony" is a first world problem of the highest order, but I see her point.

"Ah..." she sighs happily, again spreading her arms just because she can.

Glancing back at the city as we enjoy the wide open space, a vision forms in my head. Or maybe it's been there a long time, since even before I met Haley—but she's a part of it now, of course. I see us on just such a balcony, taking in this same view—but it's ours. And it's attached to a much bigger place than our apartment.

"Maybe it's time," I tell her.

"For?" she asks. But the hopeful look in her eyes makes me think we're already on the same page.

"A new place. A home with more room, and a nice space like this to sit outside on summer nights."

She looks happy but not surprised. "I've been thinking the same thing. I love Emma and Daphne to death, but we *all* need a bigger place."

Her easy agreement reminds me how in sync we generally are. "Right? I'm so glad you're on board with this." But just to be sure, I ask her, "You won't mind giving up the apartment?" It's small, but it *is* a hot property—the historic building is a popular address. "Once we give it up, we'll never get it back."

She appears wistful. "It'll always be our first home together, and the place where I carved out my adult life before you came along. And I probably won't be walking to work anymore, which *is* a nice perk. But...it's time to move on. I say the sooner the better."

I couldn't agree more. "I'm glad."

"I know a good realtor," she volunteers. "She helped Hannah and Dan find their house." It's a great home, just a few streets over from Haley's parents. "She's super nice, too. I'll get her number from Hannah."

"Sounds great," I say. "I'll call her Monday and get the ball rolling."

"We're really doing this?" she asks, timid and eager at once.

I give a brisk nod. "We're really doing this. Get ready for the home of our dreams."

Haley

Our realtor, Jacqueline, sits at one of the bakery tables with Ben, waiting for me. She's scheduled several home showings this afternoon and we couldn't be more excited. Hannah is happy to finish up for me today, so after a small rush, I wash my hands and tell my sister I'm off.

I head around the counter toward Ben and Jacqueline, untying my pink apron and whipping it off over my head as I go. "Thanks for waiting," I tell her with a smile.

"No problem," she says. "Have a seat and I'll fill you in on the places we'll be seeing today."

I slide into a café chair, all ears. "I can't wait." Ben and I both reach out to squeeze each other's hand under the table at the same time.

Jacqueline studies a propped-up tablet on the table. "As I'm sure you know, Haley," she begins, "I spoke to Ben at length on the phone Monday about your price range, neighborhoods, and what kind of home the two of you are interested in. I understand we're looking for a roomy condo with a city view."

I blink, flummoxed by her words. "We're looking for a what now?"

Even as she repeats them—"A condo with a city view"—I'm sure there's been some misunderstanding. She must have us confused with some other couple.

However, when I toss a glance to Ben, he looks completely calm and agreeable, like this makes sense to him. I'm completely astonished.

We didn't discuss what he should tell the realtor—because I didn't think we had to. Any conversation about future homes has involved, beyond more space, things like a yard, a porch, grass to mow, a backyard to entertain in.

Hasn't it?

I mean...or was it just obvious to *me*? Like the whole cat versus dog dilemma last summer.

Regardless, though, I'm stuck here, embarrassed in front of our realtor to say what I'm about to say—but I have to say it anyway. I'm not sure whether to look at her or Ben, so I end up switching my glance uncomfortably back and forth between them as I announce uncomfortably, "That's...not what I was envisioning."

At this, Ben appears even more perplexed than Jacqueline. "What do you mean?"

Of course, the completely bewildered part of me wants to blurt out, *What do you mean, what do I mean?* But for the sake of decorum, I force myself to say, politely even if totally awkwardly, "I thought we would be looking for *houses*. In *the neighborhood*." I use my hands to motion around us. "Where we live. Where we shop. Where our family is." I think of another very good—and obvious—point. "With a backyard where the dog can run and play. Along with any children we might eventually have." I'm pretty sure my eyes have widened immensely, and that I'm enunciating and possibly sounding less polite and more frustrated with each passing second.

Ben, to my utter dismay, is looking at me like I've just grown horns. "But I thought..."

Then he stops. Frustrating me further. I really want to know what on earth it is that he thought. "You thought what?"

He blinks uncertainly. "Well, I just thought for now, while we're still young...I mean, we both love a city view." It's true—taking in various city views has been "a thing" for us, and I'm well aware of how much Ben loves his cityscapes. But...

"I'm thinking about a practical, comfortable home for us, Ben. We love this neighborhood. We love being close to my parents. If we love our life here, why would we want to leave it just for a city view? I mean...the dog," I plead. "*The dog*." He, former kennel worker, knows more than most that a dog the size of Daphne needs a yard.

Yet he says to me, very calmly, "A yard can come later, babe." In a way that makes me think it would have made so much sense to have this conversation *before* the realtor was sitting here waiting to show us properties.

"Later?" I argue, losing my decorum attempt bit by bit. "I thought this would be our home for many years to come. That we'd have children in it, raise them there, all that."

Again, though, this throws him. "Really? Because I thought it would be...a starter home. A nice one—with the view and all—but a first home together. A cool place to live, right on the edge of the city. And that we'd graduate back to the suburbs...sometime down the road."

I blow out a breath, trying to wrap my head around what's happening. How can he not want what I want? We've talked about trying to get pregnant in just two or three years —and I've always envisioned that happening in some cute little cottage in the suburbs. Not in a condo without a yard! Not in the *city*!

Clearly we learned *nothing* from the whole cat/dog debacle. How did we not discuss this? Apparently when you've gone a whole year since your last disagreement, you revert to assuming you agree on everything again.

"You know what?" Jacqueline inserts, clearly seeing our mutual mounting agitation. "This happens all the time. Couples think they're on the same page and it turns out they're not. But that's okay. I can work with that."

I don't know if she's being honest or just trying to make us feel better, but her pleasant attitude helps me feel way less embarrassed. "You can?"

"Sure," she says with a reassuring smile. "If you can give me a few minutes, I'll see what else I can line up that fits in your price range and is more what you had in mind, Haley. We'll look at both cottages and condos and see where that takes us." She stands up, folding her tablet cover closed. "I'll step outside"—she points to the one small table we have on the sidewalk—"and let you two talk by yourselves for a bit."

We wait quietly as she exits, the bell on the door tinkling behind her. When she's gone, I say, "I can't believe this is happening again."

"Again?" he asks.

Is he serious? "It's like the whole dog-and-cat argument. I thought I knew what we both wanted. I thought we'd discussed it a thousand times. Now I'm thinking maybe we only discussed it in my head. But I'm also quite sure we did *not* discuss living in a condo."

He looks dubious about that, which galls me. "I feel like we have."

"Can you name some specific occasion when I said I wanted to live in a condo?"

He quickly replies, "You know I always point out the ones on the way down the hill heading into Covington and say how great the views must be and what an awesome place it would be to live."

"Yeah. So?"

"Well, you always agree."

I pull back slightly. "I do?"

He nods. "Yes."

I make a face. "I might have agreed there are probably great views. But I've never expressed wanting to live there."

"Well, when did I ever say I wanted a house in Lakeside Park?"

"A million times!" I claim.

His eyebrows shoot up in surprise.

And honestly, I'm suddenly not sure he ever said that, but... "Well, you've said at least a million times what a great neighborhood this is, and you like my parents' house and always agree what a wonderful yard they have, and you know how much I loved growing up here, so...doesn't that add up to you wanting a house here?"

He tilts his head, looking doubtful. "Maybe eventually. But not right now. Right now I'd like to come home from a long day's work and take in the view just like the other night at the hotel. I can watch my building rise up into the sky from a distance every day. I even had this idea," he goes on, clearly excited just thinking about it, "of taking a picture every day as the building goes up, and piecing them together afterward to the show the time lapse. Wouldn't that be cool?"

I nod. "Actually, it would." But then I swallow, sorry I admitted that. "Only I don't want to live in a condo."

He sighs, sounding severely let down. "We can ask Jacqueline," he says, "but I'm pretty sure any decent house with a reasonable amount of square footage *and* a city view is going to be..."

"Astronomically priced," I finish for him.

"Exactly," he says. "Whereas a condo with a view stands a better chance of being financially feasible. She has four to show us today that fit the parameters."

"*Your* parameters," I point out. "If she finds houses for us to see, too, you have to promise you'll be open-minded. And practical."

After too long of a delay for my taste, he nods. And I feel what *I* want taking away his dream. And I don't *want* to take away his dream. But I also want to honor my own vision for our home.

I can't see a way for us to both get what we want here—it's not like the dog and the cat, we can't have both. And as Jacqueline opens the door with a smile and says, "Ready to get started?" all my enthusiasm dissolves into nothing.

11

Haley

"So that's the whole stupid story," I say to Mom and Aunt Nan, sitting at a table on my parents' patio the following Saturday afternoon. The backyard is awash in color—the wisteria is still blooming, trees are billowy and green, bright petunias spill from ceramic pots suspended from the wooden slats of the pergola we're beneath. It's an amazing summer day, but I can't enjoy it because I'm in mourning that I won't have a backyard like this myself.

Dad invited Ben for a round of golf, so Mom, Nan, and I are having lunch. Finger sandwiches, macaroni salad, and watermelon, with tea cookies from the bakery for dessert. It *should* be a lovely day, but I'm ruining it by blathering on about our house-hunting dilemma.

"Well," Mom says, "how were the properties you saw? Any that could feel like a compromise?"

I shake my head, nibbling sadly on a little cookie with a pink-icing center. "We found a condo Ben loves. And I could be open to it if we, say, didn't have a dog and a cat. And didn't want kids. And if I don't mind city noise and light pollution."

Mom scrunches her nose, clearly seeing my side.

"What about the houses the realtor took you to?" Aunt Nan inquires.

I let out a wistful sigh. "There's one I liked, over on Maple. A small yellow Victorian with lots of charm and a nice wooded back. Needs a little updating, but the price was right and I could see us being happy there. If only Ben would let us. I could tell he wasn't excited about it, though. That, for him, it would feel like a consolation prize."

"Well, you can't have that," Aunt Nan says. "You need a place you both truly love."

"That seems like a tall order. Our realtor says it would be almost impossible to find a house with a city view, plus a yard and suburban feel, in our price range. It's not that they don't exist—it's that they're very pricy and rarely go on the market."

"I suppose you could stay where you are for now," Mom offers up, "and see if anything changes."

Another long sigh escapes me. "I'm so tired of tripping over pets and furniture. It was a great little place for one—but not for four. If we stay, I'm afraid it'll turn into a game of who-can't-stand-it-anymore-and-gives-in-to-the-other-person."

I nibble some more on my cookie, then take a sip of lemonade through a striped straw. "I honestly don't know what to do. I know he values that connection to the city—and yet...what about practicality? A warm, charming house, a big yard, room to start a family and give the pets some space—isn't that what makes sense here?"

Aunt Nan shrugs. "To you, of course. And to me, yes. But clearly something else makes sense to Ben, and you can't discount that, even if you don't understand it."

We all look up when Dad and Ben come strolling around the corner of the house.

"How was golf?" Mom asks.

"The kid's a natural," Dad says. It was Ben's first time playing.

That takes my thoughts to more pleasant places. "You liked it?" I ask Ben.

He shrugs, grins. "More than I expected, actually."

"Next time," Dad says, "we'll have to get Terrence out on the course with us." Dad is big on trying to hang out with Terrence as well as Ben, knowing they both lack father figures. I love how he took on that role with Ben, and even Ben's best friend, too.

Mom glances at her watch. "Later than I thought you'd be. Slow golfers in front of you?"

Ben laughs. "No, *I* was the slow one."

"That'll get better over time," Dad assures him. "And after lunch, Ben drove me by one of the places you two looked at last week."

Before I can react, Ben throws up his hands in surrender. "Not my idea. He asked, so I filled him in. He wanted to see my favorites."

I still react, though—blowing out an unhappy "Hmf."

Dad ignores this completely and says, "That view from

west Covington across the river? Breathtaking. I see the appeal."

"Et tu, Brutus?" I say resentfully to my father.

But he just laughs. "I don't think I'm all *that* bad. Like Ben says, it's not forever. If I'd had a chance to live someplace like that before your mom and I had you and your sister, I would have jumped at it."

I start blinking and shaking my head like I'm having a spasm—because my own father is actually taking Ben's side on this. Like I'm the unreasonable one.

Aunt Nan chooses that precise moment to ask, "Have you two ever opened my wedding gift?" It's not hard to see why since I'm clearly about to blow a gasket.

"Not yet," Ben says.

"Maybe it's time," she suggests.

"Maybe it is," I agree, eyes narrowed as I stare Ben down like he's the bad guy.

"Or..." Aunt Nan surprises me by continuing, "have you looked to see if there are any houses for sale on Blissful Lane?"

Ben and I just shift our gazes between each other and Aunt Nan. Suggesting a particular street might randomly have a house for sale seems odd, not to mention that it's one I'm unfamiliar with, but she said it like it was right next door. So I ask, "Where's that? It sounds directly out of a fairy tale. I've never even heard of it."

"Neither have I," my mother says. "Have you, Paul?"

"Blissful Lane?" Dad asks, screwing up his face in confusion. "Can't say that I have."

Given that we've lived in the area our whole lives, we're all a little confused.

But Aunt Nan just laughs and says, "How can you not know Blissful Lane? It's always been there. Tucked into the hillside, looking out over the river. And it might just be the answer to your problems. You never know. Ask your realtor to take a look."

Ben

The car ride home is tense. She's mad because I showed her dad the condo. She's mad about this whole thing. It's obviously not my goal to make her mad, but it's making *me* mad, too, that she won't even consider it. Most people would think it's an amazing place to live. But she's got her mind set on this one particular lifestyle for us, whether or not I'm on board.

She's right, though, that it's similar to that whole dog-or-cat problem. We haven't talked about this a lot. We've both made a lot of assumptions. And it's not like we don't talk—we talk all the time, we share everything. Except, I guess, the stuff we assume doesn't *need* sharing, like what we each want in a home.

"What do you think about Aunt Nan's suggestion?" I ask, mostly trying to thaw the deep freeze taking over the inside of the car on an otherwise hot, sunny June day.

Haley tosses me a skeptical sideways glance. "Blissful Lane? I doubt it exists."

"You think she made it up?" Sounded peculiar, I agree, but I'm surprised Haley thinks it's a total figment of her aunt's imagination.

She shrugs unhappily. "It's probably...a metaphor or something, you know? Something she's saying to help us make up."

I toss a glance *her* way now. "Are we fighting?"

She lets out a short, unsettled "Yes."

I can't argue the point, but rather than fight some more, I instead suggest, "Why don't you text the realtor. Ask her about Blissful Lane. Just for the heck of it."

She starts typing into her phone. "Fine, I'll ask. But I don't see how there can be a street around here I and my parents don't know about. I've lived here my entire life and they've lived here for all of theirs."

"It's a big area," I suggest. Though there are only so many neighborhoods with a city view.

"If it exists, all the houses are probably millions of dollars. Or...maybe she's remembering things wrong. She *is* getting older." Haley sounds sad as she says it.

And while Aunt Nan has never struck me as absent-minded or senile, she *is* a unique woman. So, again, who knows?

"I can't believe you showed Dad the condo," she suddenly spews at me.

I've actually been waiting for this since we got in the car. "He asked. Insisted, actually. It wasn't my idea, like I said."

"It made me feel ganged-up-on to have my own father not taking my side."

Ah, my sweet, innocent Haley and her sheltered life. I don't fault her, but she doesn't realize how good she's had it. To even *have* a father who might not take her side in something. To have a father nice enough to make me feel like part of the family by taking *mine*.

I won't throw that in her face, though. It's not fair to act like she's done something wrong by having a family. So instead I reply with another thought entirely, one I probably should have shared before now. It's not the kind of thing I like dredging up, but... "It might seem selfish insisting on the city view, so I've been thinking about why it's so important to me."

"I *know* why it's important to you," she says. "Your building's going to be there soon. That isn't lost on me." Her voice has gone softer now.

"I appreciate that, babe," I say, looking her way. "But there's more to it than that."

She blinks her surprise. "There is?"

"Grandpa Ed and I used to say how cool it would be to live someplace like that. We saw it as something only rich people could afford. And while you and I may not be rich, we have a lot more than Gramps ever did. And he believed in me. When I got my job, he would say, 'You're gonna get there, Ben. You're gonna get that view of the city—you mark my words.'"

"Oh," she says, her voice gone feather-light. She gets it now.

"And I know he's not here to see it," I tell her. "So maybe it's a silly reason. But, well, he was sort of like...my compass. He gave me direction. If I had an idea or a plan, and he thought it was good, it was probably good. And if he thought it was bad, it was probably bad. I had that my whole life—and without it these past few years, I've had to learn to go with my gut.

"It hasn't been easy not having that guidance—I never realized how much I depended on it until it wasn't there anymore. And so...my gut is telling me the condo on the hill feels right, and that if he were here, he'd say so, too. And maybe that *is* selfish of me—but I'm just still getting used to navigating life without him."

As I go quiet, I hate everything I just confessed. I don't want to be a man who needs a compass, who needs help. I want to be the guy I usually am: strong, decisive, has his act together. Gramps taught me to be that way. The circumstances of my life did, too. But there's no denying he's been on my mind this past week as we've dealt with this issue.

"Ben," my wife says softly, "I'm sorry. I didn't realize."

I shake my head. "It's not your fault. I didn't tell you."

"But I feel...like I should know anyway."

I absolve her. "How could you? You're not a mind reader. And I'll shake it off. I just...wanted to explain where my head is."

"I'm glad you did."

"And that doesn't make it any fairer to you. It's not a reason you should have to live someplace you don't want to."

"Just like you shouldn't have to live someplace *you* don't want to."

So...we make peace. But it doesn't come with a solution.

We stay quiet as we pull in behind our apartment building and head inside. The air feels heavy and shrouded in disappointment, for both of us.

The second we open the door, the dog is jumping on us,

the cat's meowing at our feet, and we have no room to even step around them. It's Haley who says, "We're gonna have to figure this out, though, because this apartment just isn't big enough for the four of us."

"Maybe Aunt Nan is right," I suggest.

"About the mysterious Blissful Lane?" she asks dubiously.

I laugh softly. "No. About opening the gift."

Just then, Haley's phone buzzes, and she pulls it from her purse to look. "It's Jacqueline," she tells me. "She says, *No, I'm unfamiliar with it. Where exactly is it located? Is it something you'd like me to investigate?*"

I suppose we're both a little disappointed, but not surprised. It was a long shot at best.

I look over Haley's shoulder as she types a reply: *Thanks, but no need.*

Her expression is sad as she tucks the phone back away, then looks up at me to say, "I guess maybe it *is* time to open the gift."

I know neither of us wants to open it—but it would be impossible to *ever* want to, given its purpose. Strange to want to know so badly what's inside a box, but at the same time to dread finding out.

Without further conversation, Haley goes in the other room to get the gift. I stoop to nuzzle Daphne's head and scratch behind Emma's ear, telling myself that no matter where we end up, it'll be good. Because I have Haley and these two, and really, what more do I want? Isn't a house just...the background to everything that's important?

And even if it's not what I've always seen as my ultimate

dream home, would I really be unhappy in the little yellow Victorian? Wouldn't I find it a quiet, relaxing place to come home to at the end of the day? Am I being too rigid based on a vision of what Grandpa and I saw as a sign of success? If he were here right now, what would be tell me to do? I wish I knew.

Haley

The last time I pulled this box down from the shelf, I was mad. This time I'm just sad. I had no idea this was about Ben's grandfather. Ben remains that typical guy who doesn't share everything in his head, especially when it has anything to do with the dreaded *feelings*. I've always known that, from our first date—but I sometimes forget there might be things he's not saying, lurking beneath the surface of what's obvious to me.

It strikes me now that...maybe Ben's grandpa ties in to almost everything he does in ways. Maybe I've never understood how deep Ben's losses have run.

I feel a little teary standing in front of my open closet holding Aunt Nan's gift. Would I really be unhappy in the condo? It's not the home I've envisioned, but am I being too stubborn, too selfish? Am I refusing to see the upsides?

The view *is* fabulous. It would give us way more room than we have now. The large deck would be great for entertaining. If I really want a yard, can't I just hop in the car and go to Mom and Dad's? They won't be right around the corner, but it's still a short drive. And Devou Park, the area's largest, is even closer.

But I'm still not sure.

So I carry the gift into the living room. Like a year ago, the last time we got it out, I place it on the sofa, Ben and I sitting on either side.

"You know," I say, "that whatever's in here isn't going to solve this problem."

"I know." He studies it. "I'm guessing that's not the idea of it. I'm guessing it's...something that's meant to make us feel better about *not* having an answer."

I sigh, then nod in agreement. We both peer down at the fluffy cream-colored bow, the silk flowers still artfully tucked at its center. Taking one end of the ribbon between my fingertips, I ask, "Ready?"

Another solemn nod from the man I love.

I pull at the ribbon and the bow comes loose, falling away.

And Ben says, "Haley, wait."

12

Before...

Ben

On a crisp October day, Terrence and I run through Devou Park on a paved trail that winds past an old band shell from a hundred years ago and out to vistas that overlook the city. Gold and red foliage lines our path and in places creates a canopy overhead.

"How's Olivia?" I ask. Terrence has been dating her for six months. She seems great, and it feels like she might the one for him.

"She's amazing, as usual. She just got a big promotion. I'm taking her out to dinner tonight to celebrate."

"That's awesome," I say. "Tell her I said congrats. Drinks are on me the next time we all get together."

Terrence answers all this with a nod as we run. Then asks, "Still seeing Haley?"

I am. A lot, in fact. I guess I just don't talk about it all the time. Terrence is my best friend, but also my work partner, so a lot of our daily conversations revolve around business. "Yeah. And she's good."

It earns me a sideways glance as we jog past a picnic table strewn with fallen leaves. "That's all I get. Just 'good'."

"What is it you're looking for?" I ask, slightly annoyed.

"Do you like her? Or are you getting tired of her? How much are you seeing of each other?"

Okay, it's true, I really do keep stuff to myself. And it's almost weird to realize Terrence and Haley haven't even met —something I should maybe rectify soon. But I still don't like talking about it. Maybe I don't like making a big deal of something until I'm sure it's a big deal. Although with Haley, it seems like it's going to be a big deal. Still, it's only been a few weeks. "I like her," I say.

I feel his eye roll without actually seeing it.

So I add, "I *really* like her. Okay? We see each other several times a week. We get along great and have fun together. I think we...get each other."

The next look I feel, as we reach the lot where our cars are parked, is much more approving. Terrence grabs a couple of water bottles from his backseat, tossing me one.

We sit on an old stone bench that I'm guessing has been here as long as the band shell, looking out over a golf course and the vast valley beyond. "That's good to hear, man," Terrence says. "I was beginning to worry you'd be a loner forever."

"What do you mean, a loner? I have you."

He laughs. "Yeah, but I kind of have Olivia now. And

don't take this the wrong way, but she's nicer to cuddle up with on a chilly night."

I roll my eyes and laugh. Then add, still trying to convince him—and maybe myself—that I'm not a loner, "And I was with Taryn for a while."

"I knew you'd never end up with her. She was more...for show or something."

That makes me sound shallow, but he's not wrong. When I met Taryn, I saw this chic, worldly executive type who seemed like...what I was supposed to want. I only had to date her for a few months to realize she wasn't. "Yeah, Haley's nothing like her," I say. "This girl is more...real."

"Good, man. You need that."

I pull back slightly. "I do?"

He hesitates, taking a swig from his bottle. "Well, you need *something*. Something that makes you happy beyond designing buildings. A nice girl is a good place to start." He cocks a grin my way.

But despite his good intentions, it pisses me off. Like he's saying my life sucks and I don't even know it. When, by my standards, it's pretty good. Good job, good friends, I stay healthy with running and the occasional pickup basketball game—things were going just fine before I met Haley, even if she *is* a nice addition. I draw back and cast him a sidelong look. "What do you mean, I *need* something?"

"Okay, maybe not *something*." He looks out over the rust-and-gold vista before adding, maybe reluctantly, "More like some*one*. You're not big on letting people into your life, bro."

Once again, I'm thrown. "I have plenty of people in my

life. You, Faber, Daher, Hughes, Kaeding," I say, calling some of our college buddies by their last names. "Everybody at work."

He looks unconvinced and says, "I'm talking more about people you really *let in*. Hell, you might not ever have let *me* in if we hadn't been drinking that night freshman year."

"What's your point?" I ask.

"You just don't seem to need people much. Which is fine...until you do. Like I said, I just worry you'll end up alone."

Geez—suddenly I'm a lonely old man eating a frozen dinner on a TV tray, watching infomercials and talking to houseplants.

I take that in, though, and think about what he's saying. Maybe I *don't* need people much. And maybe I see that as a *good* thing. Maybe I don't *want* to need people. "Maybe," I say, continuing my thought out loud, "I'd rather wait for the right people to come along and then *choose* them instead of just *need* them."

I think it sounds pretty damn profound, but at the same time, I know what we're both thinking. That of course a guy who's lost his whole family doesn't want to need anyone. That old cliché of being afraid to get attached to people because they all end up leaving.

And who knows—maybe it's more than a cliché. There are times when it sucks not to have any family. But I don't sit around analyzing my life that way.

Terrence finally cuts me a break, saying, "Well, if you're digging on this girl and she's digging on you, I'm glad, man."

"Me, too." Simple as that.

Then he looks over at me. "So, is it, like, serious?" Quickly seeing that he's annoyed me again already, rather than stop, instead he hams it up, enunciating in a way he clearly thinks is hilarious as he goes on. "Is it *exclusive*? Is it a *committed relationship*?"

Still, I keep my reply light, and true. "I'm just living in the moment here, dude. Just having fun, taking it day by day."

And, in fact, I appreciate that Haley isn't pressuring me to make a commitment. It's easier than that between us—pretty effortless, honestly. Maybe that's one of the reasons I'm into her.

The truth is, my grandpa's death laid me low for a while. But at the same time it forced on me a strength and independence I couldn't have gotten any other way. I bounced back and actually learned to like life on my own, with no one to answer to or worry about or share the remote with. I came to appreciate doing my own thing. Taryn showed me that big time—breaking up with her was like starting to breathe again after months of feeling smothered, and it made me like being alone even more.

And then came Haley, out of the blue, when I least expected it. Who knows—if I'd wandered into the bakery any other day besides the one where I was in an unusually good mood, maybe I wouldn't have been so friendly, and maybe she wouldn't have reminded me we'd met before, and maybe I wouldn't be doing anything tonight but going home to watch TV. Would I be happier that way?

No. Hell no.

I say to Terrence next to me on the bench, "If it makes you feel any better, I can't wait to see her tonight."

Terrence lets out a triumphant laugh and slaps me on the back.

Haley

The first Saturday of November is a beautiful day full of bright sun, blue skies, and crisp air. Ben and I are picnicking on a quilt at the Devou Park Overlook—with one of the best views of Cincinnati you can find. He made sandwiches, and I brought pumpkin pie from the bakery, along with a thermos of hot apple cider.

It's a busy day at the overlook—there's a farmer selling pumpkins from the back of an old red pickup and a Girl Scout troop is selling apple pies and turnovers. A few guys with guitars strum in the gazebo to our right.

Some people, like us, are just hanging out—others come and go to take in the view for a few minutes from the benches at the bottom of the hill where we've spread our blanket. It's a veritable parade of sweaters, puffy vests, and cozy scarves. Fallen leaves scatter the ground like orange and yellow confetti, but the trees are still reluctant to let some of them go.

Yet the thing that colors all of this for me even more than the fall leaves is...I'm crazy about him. My heart beats faster at the very notion of him. He's the first thing I think about when I wake up and the last thing on my mind as I fall asleep at night.

Things between us are easy, fun, casual. So while I don't try to hide how much I like him, at the same time I play it at least a little bit cool. Meaning I haven't blurted out the 'L' word or anything. The whole pressure of the 'L' word—who says it first, and when, and how—I hate the weight of those questions. But I have a history of saying it first, at the wrong time, in the wrong way—so it does hold weight.

I'm not thinking about that, though, as I soak up the splendor of a beautiful autumn afternoon with the guy I'm falling for. Later, we'll head to Ben's place to order pizza and watch movies. We've hung out at my apartment a few times now, but this will be my first time at his.

"What a beautiful day," I say to the insanely handsome guy next to me.

"Perfect," he replies with a smile that suggests I'm part of what's making it that way. My chest warms, along with my cheeks.

"Seems like you come here a lot," I remark. He's mentioned that he runs here sometimes.

"Lot of good trails," he tells me, "and you can't beat this view."

We both look out at the city. He definitely has a thing about that, the skyline. Since taking me to Riverside Drive on our first date, we've viewed the city from other spots as well.

As if reading my mind, he offers up an almost self-deprecating laugh. "I probably seem like some country bumpkin who can't stop looking at the big city."

I tilt my head. "Despite your history, I would never call you a country bumpkin." If he ever came across that way, he must have long since banished that from his personality, and he has no trace of a rural accent whatsoever. "On that first day we met in the cemetery, I thought you were way more cosmopolitan than, say, me. Or most people."

"I guess it's something I worked at for a while. To be taken seriously in my classes at UC, and then later, at my job. Some people really judge a person's intelligence or competence based on that kind of thing. I don't think about it much lately, though."

"I guess you really became that guy," I say. "Or always were and just didn't know it."

He's still focused on the view, though. "This probably comes from growing up in the country where there weren't many people, but part of what I love about the city is...when I look at it I can't help thinking of all the thousands upon thousands of people who've lived there, or worked there, who've traveled the streets from back when they were brick right up to now."

I smile. "I suspect that not growing up here gives you a more unique perspective than the rest of us have."

"I've always been fascinated by cities—I even loved TV shows set in various cities as a kid, because they're so different from where I lived. My world felt small in comparison. Most people where I come from can't understand why anyone would move to the city, why they'd leave rolling hills and fresh air. And I get that. But at the same time, the energy of the city just gets inside me."

"You're making me see it through new eyes," I tell him, captivated by his mind.

"What was it like growing up here," he asks, "with the city just a few miles away?"

Turning it over in my head, I answer honestly. "I'm sorry to say I guess it's something I've taken for granted. Don't get me wrong—I love this view, too. And I like taking advantage of all the city has to offer—the arts, festivals, restaurants—but it's always just...been there. In my backyard, so to speak. Just a hop, skip, and a jump away from my nice, quiet neighborhood. It's always seemed like the best of both worlds. This might sound crazy, but I truly can't think of anyplace I'd rather live than Lakeside Park."

"Well, not crazy," he says, absolving me with a smile, "but that's a big statement."

"I suppose it makes me lucky. My parents' house is perfect to me—on a winding street, with a huge backyard and a pond. You can open the windows on summer nights and hear the crickets. Which," I stop and check myself, realizing, "is probably nothing to you. Where you're from, I suppose anyone can open the windows and hear the crickets. But as close to the city as my parents' place is, it's kind of an added value." I finish on a short laugh.

"I guess we all can take things for granted. And the grass really is greener on the other side. It sounds like a great place, though."

"It is," I tell him, unsure why I'm so eager to convince him—but I guess that house, that neighborhood, is just a part of me. "I'd love to show you where I grew up sometime. You could meet Aunt Nan again—she's over at my parents' place a lot. And Puff." I've told him all about Puff, of course. And this next part was planned, but not for right now—and yet here it is, spilling out of my mouth. "Would you like to come to Thanksgiving at my Mom and Dad's?"

He hesitates.

And my heart drops like a stone, just from that. He's never hesitated before, about any plans we've ever made.

Finally, he says, "Can I let you know?"

"Sure," I say quickly. Even though I'm dying inside.

And also wondering what better he has to do—this man with no family. I thought I was giving him someplace to go. A family experience to be a part of. A way to feel included in a holiday he might otherwise spend alone.

I draw my eyes from his, suddenly more thankful for the great view—it's something else to look at.

"I appreciate the invitation," he says.

Things have turned awkward now. I might as well have grass stain on my shirt and twigs in my hair.

"I'm just not used to a big family thing," he goes on.

"Of course," I answer. "It's no biggie." But it *is* a biggie—it's a hugie. Because I've put myself out there, trusting this would be as easy as everything else between us so far.

And maybe I should be more sympathetic—maybe Thanksgiving dredges up feelings of loss for him or something. But if it does, I want to know, and I want to fix that, change that. Does he not *want* to be part of a family? And maybe it's too soon to be thinking about that, or even too soon to be inviting him to Thanksgiving—but we see each other all the time, he has no family, and we seem to be pretty crazy about each other, so I followed my heart, never dreaming he'd do anything but happily accept.

Conversation goes on—he's suddenly working hard to *make* it go on. Because he knows I'm embarrassed now and he's trying to repair that. But it's not working; my brain is spinning. And I've put up a wall, that quick. I'm suddenly distant, giving short replies, and peering off into that skyline like it holds the secrets to the universe.

And maybe I'm overreacting. But I've been here before and I know how this goes. It starts with one little hesitation, but then it grows, and it turns into chasing, into me thinking something I say or do will magically convince this guy he *does* want what I want—when he just plain doesn't. I heard it in his voice—it wasn't an honest, conflicted 'can I get back to you?' It was a putting on of brakes. A 'whoa, Nelly.' A 'this is moving too fast.' I thought it *was* moving pretty fast, for both of us. But if we're suddenly not going the same speed, that's a bad sign.

"Are you mad at me?"

I flit a glance his way. "What? No, don't be silly." I look back to the city before us, now kind of wishing I could just somehow disappear into it.

"Haley? Haley Munson, is that you?"

I lift my head to find a woman peering down on me, and I'm struggling to figure out who she is when she touches a palm to her chest and reminds me, "I'm Kirby's mom, Sherry."

Kirby's mom. Kirby, who broke my heart and made me feel like a heaping pile of nothing. What fresh hell have I descended into? "Hi," I murmur. "Um, how is he?" I don't *want* to ask about him, but even as fraught as I am at the moment, the Midwestern people pleaser inside me does it anyway.

"Well, it's tough in New York. Very expensive," she says. "But he's gotten some gigs in bars and coffee shops, and he seems happy."

"That's great," I say. Even though I still resent him and I'm not sure I mean it.

"I'll tell him you said hi."

I didn't and wish you wouldn't. But I hold that in and instead say, "Okay."

"It was nice to see you."

"You, too," I lie. It's actually been incredibly awkward, which is probably why she cut it blessedly short. The only good I can find in the whole scenario is that at least she saw me with a hot guy, which she might mention to her wayward son.

As Kirby's mother walks away, I say, "Ex-boyfriend's mom," and roll my eyes.

"Bad breakup?" Ben asks.

"You could say that," I reply, and leave it at that.

But then I decide *not* to leave it at that. I decide not to play anything cool anymore, come what may. Because I'm a sharer—maybe not everyone is, but I am. And because if Ben doesn't want to come for Thanksgiving, maybe in the end we won't be well-suited. Maybe in the end he won't like me for me—and I just want someone I can be me with.

And so I be me. "I thought we were serious, but he dumped me to move to New York and pursue a career in music. I was crushed. And I followed that up with another toxic relationship that ended badly."

"Um, how long ago?" I can't read his expression or know what he's thinking about all this because I'm not looking at him.

"The last one ended several months before I met you. Which is to say—I was *not* in the market for romance when Aunt Nan sent me trudging up the hill toward you in the cemetery. I was taking a break. I planned for it to be a long one."

"Guess that makes me lucky then," he says. "That you even gave me the time of day."

"Guess so," I say, meeting his gaze for the first time in a while. What I'm saying to him silently in that moment: *You're not the only one afraid of things.* Since I know he is. He's afraid of getting attached to a family when he's gotten used to being without one. And I'm afraid of getting attached to another guy who's going to toss me away like an old, worn-out pair of sneakers. Then I point over my shoulder, up the hill toward the restrooms. "I'll be back in a minute."

I have no idea what I'm doing at this point. No idea why I told him what I just told him. No idea what it says about me —to me or to him. No idea if I'm overreacting to his reticence about Thanksgiving. No idea if he's the guy I've—probably naively—thought he is the past two months. After all, I don't have a great track record in that department. I've been known to see what I want to see.

So I go to the bathroom and text Hannah. I ask her to text me back in a few minutes. I say I'm going to tell Ben she has some kind of emergency and needs me to watch the kids tonight. Because I don't think I want to go to his place after all. I want to cut this date short, end the awkwardness I created, and think this through.

Her response: *What???? Why? What's wrong?*

I saw a relationship red flag today, I reply.

And you're ending the date due to one flag? she asks.

I remind her: *I usually ignore the flags and it doesn't go well for me. I'm trying to be smart here. Trying to protect myself for a change.*

She says: *I hate this. I thought he was going to be special.*

Me, too. And maybe I'm overreacting. But I don't want to spend the whole night wondering while I'm with him. I need some time to be alone, reassess.

She accepts that. *Okay. I'll text shortly.*

When I exit the bathroom, the day feels less beautiful, and like winter is coming. I quietly rejoin Ben on our quilt. I have nothing to say.

"Listen," he tells me softly, the very tone of his voice drawing my gaze to his. "I'm sorry I acted weird when you invited me to Thanksgiving. I'd love to come. I'd love to meet your family."

My heart inflates, and I'm utterly stunned by the turnaround. "You would? Really?" Then I look down. "Because I don't want you to do anything you don't want to—"

He touches my arm to shut me up. "I do want to. Promise." Then he shakes his head. "I think I just...needed a minute to adjust to the idea. I haven't been to many big family Thanksgivings. Even as a kid, it was just my parents and grandparents—that was it. Since Grandpa died, I've just ignored it altogether. It's a weird day for me."

Okay, so now I feel like a jerk. "I'm sorry," I say. "I should have considered that more."

But he shakes his head again. "I can't expect you to know everything going on in my brain when I don't tell you."

"You...*can* tell me stuff, you know. If you want."

He nods. "I'll get better at that."

Just then, my phone buzzes and I look at it. Hannah. I

don't even read the text—I just type back: *Crisis averted. Sorry for the drama.*

And that fast, it really is.

I can't bring his family back, but I can make him feel like he belongs somewhere if he'll let me. I think he belongs...with me. City, suburbs, country—who cares? I'm sort of starting to think that Ben just feels like...home to me.

13

Back to the Wedding Box

Ben

I touch Haley's hand and remind her of something she once said to me early in our relationship. "Home is wherever we are together."

She smiles. "I was just thinking about that, too. I was thinking about the day when I invited you to Thanksgiving."

"And I almost blew it." Then I raise suggestive eyebrows. "But remember what else happened that day? That night actually."

"How could I forget?"

It was the first time we spent the night together. The memory makes me lean over and kiss her, then say, "Before we open the box, let's just do one thing. Let's find out if Blissful Lane even exists."

We should have before now—it just sounded too...made-up. Especially since our real estate agent has never heard of it, either. But I pull out my phone and Google it.

Then blink my surprise as it pops up on my screen. "It exists."

I glance up in time to see Haley's jaw drop. "Where?"

I'm even more shocked as I tell her, "Near Devou Park."

"Let's go," she says. "I doubt it's going to solve all our home woes, but let's just go and see what this mysterious Blissful Lane is all about."

We close up the dog and the cat in the apartment and hop in the car. I'm driving—Haley uses her phone to navigate once we reach the general area. There are million-dollar-plus homes near the park—and a lot of that price tag is about the location. We can't afford the houses we're driving past, but neither of us is bothering to say it. Blissful Lane might exist, but it won't be feasible. And houses in this neighborhood seldom go up for sale anyway.

"It says to turn left in a thousand feet," she tells me, "but I don't think there are any streets off this one."

"Yeah, it ends right up here." It's a dead-end with a home directly where the street stops.

But then I notice a narrow paved lane to the left of that house, mostly obscured by a canopy of trees. "It can't be *that*, can it?" I ask. "Looks like a private driveway."

"Surely not," she replies, then looks back down at her phone. "But on the map, sort of seems like that's it. Drive closer."

I do, and only when the nose of the car is practically up under the trees do we both spot a little wooden street sign, mostly covered by greenery, but the word "BLISS" can be seen.

"How can that be a street?" I ask. "I run past here sometimes and I've never seen it."

"I've lived here *my whole life* and never seen it," Haley says. Then we look at each other—before proceeding slowly down Blissful Lane.

After just a few car lengths the street widens a little, but it's still a narrow path through the trees that reminds me more of my rural Kentucky past than a place within eyesight of a major city. A sharp curve to the right reveals a couple of houses on small plateaus carved into the hillside, but still surrounded by trees. We both ooh and ahh a little when we spy the city views behind the houses, one of which is an older but grand-looking Tudor, popular around the park, and the other a modern ranch house.

After that, more tree-lined drive—until the car emerges into a clearing and we both spot the most amazing sight. "Is that a For Sale sign?" Haley asks, squinting through the windshield. "That can't be a For Sale sign."

"No," I say, "it can't. Except I think it is."

That's when we roll up on a pretty white house with lacy gingerbread trim. Tucked into the steep hillside, it still has an ample backyard with that same stunning city view. It rocks a cottage vibe, but it's not small—one and a half stories at a glance, with what I suspect is a full basement.

We're both stunned into silence as I stop the car. How can this be here? This perfect-looking home for sale in this perfect spot that no one knows exists? Well, besides Aunt Nan. My heart is pounding and I'm sure Haley's is, too, but before we get too far ahead of ourselves, I feel the need to state the obvious. "We'll never be able to afford it." Houses in this area with this view are way out of our price range—even average ones. The condos we're looking at are farther away and at the top of our budget.

"You're right," she says, sounding a little defeated.

We both let out tired sighs. I'm almost sorry we've come. It felt like a little adventure, a desperate search for magic to delay the opening of the box. Part of me thought we'd find out the street was on private property, or uninhabitable. Even when we found it, I didn't quite imagine my dream view, or Haley's dream house, or that both of them would be for sale but surely out of our reach.

"There's a sales sheet," she says, pointing to the little metal box attached to the sign. Which strikes me as odd actually—how many random drive-bys is this place going to get? It's within sight of the city, but at the same time in the middle of nowhere.

Haley gets out and walks over, grabbing a flyer. And even from my place in the driver's seat, I see her eyes go wide. She comes running up to my door, thrusting the sheet of paper at me as I lower the window. "Look at this!"

Taking it from her, I find that the house is almost in our price range, just a little beyond it. Which seems impossible. But in bold at the top it says: ***Priced for quick sale! Motivated seller!***

This propels me out of the car—I need to take a better look at this place.

"We should call Jacqueline," Haley says.

And that's when my phone rings and I look down. "This is her now." I answer by saying, "Funny timing—we were literally just about to call you."

"Really? Well, I'm calling to tell you about a brand new listing. On your mysterious Blissful Lane of all places!"

"We're standing in front of it right now," I inform her.

"Oh. Wow. Does it look vacant?"

I glance around. No cars. No plants or chairs on the front porch. "I think so."

"Hold on a sec," she says. Then comes back a minute later to tell me she was able to schedule a showing for right now. "I'll be there in fifteen minutes. But first I'm going to text the selling agent to let him know I have serious interest. I don't want anyone swooping in on this. See you shortly."

"She's on her way," I tell Haley with a smile as I hang up.

"This is it," she declares. "I already know. My skin is tingling. This is our new home."

The sensible part of me wants to argue. I want to warn her there could be problems inside we can't see yet. Maybe we'll hate the interior. A million things could be wrong.

But deep inside, I know it's not true. Deep inside, I know we won't be opening Aunt Nan's gift today, after all.

I know it even more when Haley, already circling the house quicker than I can keep up, says, "Ben, oh my God. Come look. Come look!"

When I reach the back, I'm wowed by the perfection of the skyline view. But Haley is focused on something else. A flower bed. "Daisies!" she says. "There are daisies!"

14

Haley and Ben's Three-Year Anniversary

Haley

Aunt Nan always says you should never let fear guide your decisions. But I'll be honest—right now I'm a little scared. I mean, it wouldn't be the end of the world. It's just not how we planned it. And while no one would claim I'm the master of plan-following, when it comes to big stuff, maybe I am. You don't run a business without the ability to follow a plan. When it comes to some things, I'm very spontaneous, but with others, I value sticking to the plan. And I value having a husband who commonly *makes* those plans. That's one more thing I love about our marriage—Ben enjoys being the plan-maker and I enjoy being off-the-hook in that way.

That's what's on my mind as I host a cookout at our house on Blissful Lane. Ben and Dad are playing cornhole in the distance with Terrence and Olivia. Hannah, Dan, and Aunt Nan are manning the grill while Sienna and I put together a fruit salad. I've hollowed out half a watermelon as a bowl to hold the fruit and am feeling very Martha Stewart about it. Mom is blowing bubbles with Cora and Cole, and Sienna stops to spontaneously grab her camera and snap pictures of them because downtown Cincinnati is providing the perfect backdrop. "There," she says, returning to the picnic table to pick back up her fruit-chopping knife. "You can frame one of these and have an amazing Christmas gift for your parents."

"See why I love you?" I say to her. More than once, her ability to capture the everyday as a work of art has provided me with the perfect gift for someone I love, and our own home overflows with photos Sienna has taken.

The house is amazing. And the cookout is an unofficial thank you to our friends and family for all the moving and painting and other help they've given us this past year. Later we'll toast marshmallows and make s'mores over the firepit Terrence and Ben built last fall.

"No no," I say to Daphne as she comes begging for food. "You don't like fruit anyway, and you have your own delicious dinner in your bowl. It's not my fault you're ignoring it." Daphne is still in training two years after coming to live with us, but such is life with a rescue dog. Overall, she's still a wonderful pet and loves having a yard to play in.

Unlike Puff, Emma doesn't come outside—strictly an indoor kitty—but I see her curled in a windowsill, soaking up a burst of late day sun while she looks out on her people.

Life is good. Darn near perfect, in fact. Except for the pesky thing I'm a little worried about right now.

I carry the big watermelon fruit bowl to the food table, adding it to a spread of baked beans, potato salad, deviled eggs, and more. Looks like the cornhole game has concluded since Ben is heading my way across the patio. "Who won?" I ask.

"Olivia and your dad kicked our butts," he says, laughing. "Heading in to wash up before dinner."

I nod, still arranging the food, happy but at the same time slightly distracted.

Instead of continuing toward the back door, Ben touches my shoulder. "Hey, something wrong?"

I have no idea how he knows. But then, I guess he knows me better than anyone. And maybe I'm a little quieter than normal, more watching the event than taking part in it. "Not really," I claim anyway.

Of course, he looks doubtful. "You seem a little off, not quite yourself."

Well, if he's going to be all super-perceptive about it, I may as well just tell him. "I'm a little late, that's all."

"Late for what?" he asks. Such a man response. He might be perceptive, but still a man.

I whisper, "My period." Then proceed in a more normal tone of voice. "But I'm sure it's fine. I'm just usually like clockwork. Though I'm sure it's fine and I'll start any time now."

I can't quite decipher the look on his face. He's taking it in, weighing it. Then he squeezes my arm and says softly, "Hey, either way, it'll be okay. All right?"

Well, of course he's going to say that, because either way, it *has* to be okay. "I know," I tell him. "But I like our five-year plan."

"I do, too. Still, don't worry."

The five-year plan was a much looser, unnamed thing until we bought the house. We adore the house, and certainly couldn't pass up such a house—but it was slightly beyond our budget, so Ben suggested "the five-year plan," meaning we start trying to have babies around our fifth anniversary. We moved here just two years after we got married—which was a year ago already. So there are two more to go before baby time. And this is one plan I want to stick to, for many reasons.

"Burgers hot off the grill," Dan says, approaching with a platter.

"Hotdogs coming up, too," Hannah announces from where she's forking them from the grill onto a plate.

Ben ends the conversation by giving me a quick wink and heading inside. I feel better having filled him in. And now I resolve to enjoy the rest of the day without worry. I can worry tomorrow if I need to.

Ben

Haley's "lateness" stays on my mind the rest of the day—there's suddenly not room for anything else in my brain. Everyone is sitting around talking about how delicious Aunt Nan's deviled eggs are, or who's going to take on Olivia and Haley's dad in cornhole after we eat, or how fabulous the view is—but I'm still busy wondering if it's really possible she's pregnant.

We've loosely discussed making the two rooms on the second floor kids' rooms, but now I'm thinking in a more immediate way—like that my office makes more sense as a nursery, even though we just finished making it an office, because it's closer to our room. And is a firepit dangerous for a toddler? How will the dog be with a baby? Daphne's very gentle, but a baby adds a whole new element to the equation.

That evening after dark, I'm sitting in the living room watching TV, but really studying the stone fireplace. We love the fireplace, but now I'm thinking about baby-proofing it, and wondering how you teach a baby that fire burns—but at the same time realizing the mantle is a perfect place for Christmas stockings and what a great house this will be for a kid to grow up in.

That's when Haley comes buzzing into the room, beaming. "Good news! I was right—it was a false alarm. Just a random bit of lateness, I guess."

"Oh. Wow. Okay," I say. I don't know why it surprises me, but it does.

"So *that's* a big relief," she declares.

And I hear these words come out of my mouth. "Is it?"

She drops onto the couch adjacent to my easy chair. "Well, of course. We're not ready for that. Not yet."

"I know," I say, nodding, but inside I'm thinking: *Do* I know? *Aren't* we ready?

"Why do you look weird?"

I blink, sigh, trying to figure that out. The truth is, I'm still absorbing the blow. That she's not pregnant. And that it *is* a blow. An actual blow. "I...think I'm disappointed."

She sits up straighter. "What?"

"I just realized that when you said you might be pregnant, I wished it were true."

She *whooshes* out a long breath, thrown by my reaction. Which I understand. Though at the same time, I find myself suggesting, "You know, we *could* drop the birth control and let nature take its course. Just see what happens."

She slumps a bit, abject worry overtaking her expression. "But what about our plan? It's a good plan. A plan we devised for a reason. Lots of reasons, in fact."

"I know, but..."

I don't have to formulate an end to that thought, since she keeps going. "And who *are* you? Newsflash—I'm the impulsive, spontaneous one here. You're the careful planner. I *like* having a careful planner to balance me out."

It's true. This is a total role reversal. If you'd asked me six months ago how such a scenario would play out, I'd have thought *she'd* be the one to suddenly want a baby and I'd be hammering home the plan. "Look," I say, "I'm as thrown by this as you. I didn't see it coming at all. Until it was suddenly...a thing that might be happening. And I *liked* that it might be happening. So...maybe we *don't* have to stick to the plan."

"I thought we were saving money," she argues. "Fixing up the house up exactly the way we want it, and then saving. In case I want to work less for a few years after a baby comes along. I thought we were making sure we had all the pieces in place."

All true. "But it would all work out," I assure her.

"How do you know?"

"Because things always do." It's not a profound answer, but a valid one, I think.

"That sounds like *my* crazy logic and I don't like it—not one bit."

That makes me laugh—but then I get more serious.

"Haley, I want to have a baby with you. Doesn't that make you happy? I mean, there was a time when..."

"Yes, a time when you were worried about that kind of big life commitment. So of course it makes me happy. I'm just saying I'm very comfortable with our plan. Which means baby time is two years away."

I press my lips flat, choosing my response carefully. What I finally come to is, "That suddenly sounds like a long time to wait."

But she's unmoved. "I'm twenty-eight. You're thirty-one. We have so much time. And it flies by in a flash, in case you haven't noticed. Two years will pass in the blink of an eye."

"I know all that," I tell her. "I guess I'm just suddenly... ready."

She blinks, clearly confounded by my pushiness, then speaks through slightly clenched teeth. "But. The. Plan."

"I know I'm throwing you a curveball. And I know it's not fair. But, again, I'm just saying we could see what happens without birth control. That's all."

"That's not what we agreed on," she reminds me, suddenly going impudent.

"I'm asking you to just think about it. Be open to it."

Her response is to get up and leave the room. "I'm going to take a shower," she says over her shoulder as she exits. Which doesn't sound very open.

And I just sit there, surprised by how crushed I am. She's right—who am I? I don't really recognize myself right now, either.

Haley

I'm at the cemetery with Aunt Nan, decking out Uncle Philip's grave for the Fourth of July. We've placed red gardenias in pots wrapped in red foil, and stuck star-spangled pinwheels in the ground. I'm tying grosgrain ribbons in the tree branches above while Aunt Nan pokes holes in the red foil and lowers them halfway into the ground in holes we've prepared—both to help them soak up groundwater and keep them from tipping over.

"Your Uncle Philip loved the Fourth of July," she declares.

"Really?" I glance down at where she kneels before the headstone. "I never knew that."

"You don't remember how we took you girls to every fireworks display? And how he always brought you and Hannah pinwheels like these?"

"I do remember," I say, thinking back. "I just didn't realize it was a love for the holiday so much as a way to have fun."

"He was a very patriotic man and always reminded me how lucky we were to be Americans." She tilts her head then, appearing to travel back in time. Then a slight smile steals over her, along with a shrug of her shoulders. "Myself, I could take or leave the fireworks—they're pretty, I suppose, but always so loud, and I feel like once you've seen one display, you've seen them all."

Another revelation for me. "I thought you always liked it just as much as he did."

"I liked having an activity with my husband and nieces.

And sometimes in a marriage you pretend a little, you work to see things from the other person's angle—and you either come to see it their way, or you don't but you act like you do. Now, don't get me wrong," she goes on, using a pinwheel as a pointer, "I'm not saying you never sacrifice yourself—I'm just saying you remember you're in a partnership where each person's views are valid, and you be a good partner when you can."

"Ben wants to have a baby," I blurt out. "Like right now."

Aunt Nan draws back her chin, stunned by my announcement. "That's not the plan."

"Thank you," I tell her emphatically. "That's what I keep reminding him."

"What brought this on?"

"I was late. Only by a few days, but enough to make me wonder. Apparently it was enough to make him want a baby, plan be damned."

I can see her turning this over in her head. "It's not like Ben to deviate from a plan."

"Thank you again," I say. "I'm flabbergasted by it. But he keeps asking me to consider not waiting. And he doesn't seem to be letting it go."

"How do you feel about that?"

I think I've made that pretty clear already, but I tell her, "I prefer to stick to the plan. I prefer having another couple of years for just the two of us. I prefer being able to save some money."

"What if your false alarm hadn't been a false alarm? How would you feel then?"

I think that through. "Well, I'd adjust. I'd be adjusting. I'd have to embrace the idea."

She smiles at me. "Then maybe that's your solution. Adjusting."

I tilt my head, casting a doubtful look. I feel like I'm being tricked. "This is a little bigger than pretending to like fireworks."

"Of course it is," she agrees. "I'm just saying that sometimes, in a marriage, there are moments, even big ones, when you have to put the other person's wants ahead of your own if you possibly can."

"And you're saying this is one of those times?" Frankly, this surprises me. Aunt Nan wants everyone to be happy, but she would normally never suggest a woman let a man talk her into something.

"I'm just suggesting you think about it," she replies, now looking back down at her task, adjusting flowerpots. "Things happen for a reason and maybe this is happening for a reason, too. And...well, if your Uncle Philip and I had ever been able to have a baby, we would have leaped on that opportunity, whenever and however it occurred."

I let out a long sigh, my heart suddenly aching. Because... "I never knew you really wanted that. I mean, I knew you couldn't, but I didn't know you wanted it."

She looks up at me, wide-eyed. "Oh, we did. Very much. It's not the kind of sadness you dump on your beloved nieces, but we really did."

My heart breaks for her. Even if it's not something you dump on your niece, I still wish she'd told me before now. This conversation is making me realize how much we don't always know about our elders, how much they choose not to share, and yet it was there all along, even though we thought we knew them so well. I'm grateful my aunt and uncle had Hannah and me to lavish their love on, and I'm grateful we had them, too.

"Maybe I'm just...a little afraid," I confess. I'm not sure I knew this until right now, but when I dig deeper into my feelings, that's what I come to. "Of change. Of...I don't know—aren't there are a million things to be afraid of when it comes to having babies?"

"You know what I always say about fear."

"I do. In fact, I thought about that while I was waiting for my period to start."

She looks pleased to know her advice really does have an impact on me. "However," she says, "only you can resolve this one, dear—you and you alone."

That day on the way home, I stop at the drugstore and pick up my birth control prescription. I don't even think about it in relation to this—I just pick it up, because it's there and I *always* pick it up.

What I don't expect is Ben's reaction when sees the little pharmacy bag on the kitchen counter that night.

"So I see nothing has changed," he remarks.

He's just come in from work and looks tired. He's had a long day, so I—wisely, I think—suggest, "Is this really the time to discuss it?"

"Well, if you're about to start another month of it, yes."

"I can quit any time I want," I tell him.

"I'm not accusing you of being an addict—I'm just saying

it seems like you don't plan to if you paid for a new prescription."

"I think you're in a bad mood and maybe we should discuss this later."

"What does it matter? It's going to turn out the same way —now, later, next week, next month."

"I don't think you're being fair."

He shrugs. "Maybe not. I just can't believe my wife doesn't want to have a child with me."

My eyes widen in outrage. "What a mean, horrible accusation! That's a low blow. You're not fighting fair here."

He stops, sighing, and runs a hand back through his hair. "Maybe you're right. But that's just how it feels."

"Well, it's not true," I insist. And now I'm mad, too. We fight so rarely—I'm not sure we're good at it. It always sneaks up on us. I'm not used to the emotions it riles up inside me. I instantly long for peace—and only one thought for at least *reaching* toward that comes to mind. "And you know what? If ever there was a time to open Aunt Nan's wedding present, I'd say it's now. Because we're both mad and we're both hurt. So how about it? Shall we finally see what on earth is in that stupid box that she somehow thinks is going to make everything better?"

"Fine," he snaps. "You want to open it—let's open it."

"Fine," I return. "I'll go get it right now."

"I'm gonna go outside and have a beer. Maybe the view will calm me down."

He's not a big drinker—only socially. I don't think I've ever known him to open a beer to relieve stress, and it irks me all the more. "Great—I'll meet you and your beer on the patio with the gift!"

A few minutes later, I stomp out the back door onto the flagstone and find Ben, still in his shirt and tie, in one of two Adirondack chairs facing the river. I plop down in the other and pretty much slam the pretty box onto the small table between us.

"Ready?" I ask sharply.

"Ready," he nearly growls.

And that's when Daphne appears out of nowhere behind us, and before I can register what's happening, she reaches up, grabs the box's ribbon in her mouth, and goes running away with the gift!

"Oh my God, are you serious?" I mutter. I don't even know who I'm talking to—Ben? The dog? God himself?

"I didn't even know she was out here," he grumbles.

We both watch as Daphne frolics merrily to and fro across the backyard with Aunt Nan's wedding gift dangling from her teeth—she thinks it's a toy and that we're all having fun here.

"Who's chasing this time?" I ask, unable to believe yet another dog has to be chased at this pivotal moment in our relationship.

"I'll do it," Ben says.

15

Before...

Ben

I'm driving Haley to her parents' house for Thanksgiving, aware of how much I don't want to go, even though I'm crazy about her. It's not about her, or even her family. It's because I've been down this road before. The holiday-invite road.

For years after my parents were killed, someone always invited Gramps and me over for Thanksgiving or Christmas dinner. Friends or neighbors, all kind people concerned about making us feel loved and not alone. The only problem was—it never failed to dredge up for us all we'd lost, and that we *were* alone. Everyone meant well—they always do. But there's no way to get through those days without being reminded I've never had a big family, and that even my small family didn't last very long.

After Grandpa Ed moved in with me, Terrence insisted we come to his family's house for holidays. We didn't want to refuse the kindness, so we went. But the same as when I was a kid, every time we left, it was a relief. Gramps would even joke about it. "Well, we made it through, Ben. Now we can finally go home and relax." Only he wasn't really joking—he'd say it with a smile, but it came with tired eyes.

I agreed to Haley's family Thanksgiving because that day in the park I could feel her pulling away, putting up a barrier. She caught me off guard and I responded with my gut. I had plenty of reasons to say no, but the threat of losing her, over a dinner, changed my mind in an instant. And so off we go. But all in all, I'd rather be at home in my apartment heating up a frozen pizza and watching football.

In the short drive from her place to theirs, I see the neighborhood is everything she promised. Large trees with a few last determined leaves still clinging to branches, sizable homes rich with character, big yards on winding streets. The house Haley grew up in would fit well on a breezy Maine coastline with a barn-shaped gambrel roof and cedar shake lining the gables. It looks warm and inviting.

"That's my room," she says merrily, pointing at a small oval window above a large, curving porch. She sounds suddenly girlish, excited for me to see this part of her life, and it's hard not to be charmed by her. I always am, after all.

We look to be among the last to arrive judging by the number of cars in the driveway, and I brace myself for a flurry of introductions as we let ourselves in the front door without knocking.

As expected, it's a whirlwind of activity inside—people moving busily around the kitchen, someone setting a long table in the open-concept space that connects the kitchen to a family room. The aroma of a baking turkey fills the air. There's football on a big TV, and a couple of little kids running around.

"That's my dad, Paul, and my sister's husband, Dan," Haley says, pointing into the TV area, "and my niece and nephew, Cora and Cole." Then she pivots back toward the kitchen. "You know Hannah from the bakery." I lift my hand in a wave as Hannah looks up from placing neatly rolled pumpkin-colored cloth napkins atop each plate. "And that's my mother, Nina, and Aunt Nan at the stove."

Everyone tosses out hellos. Haley's mother is saying, "It's so nice to meet you, Ben—we're so happy you're joining us today," and her dad is inviting me into the family room, offering me a beer and asking if I'm a football fan.

As I shake Paul's hand, I inform him I am, adding, "I try to get to a Bengals' game every once in a while," though even as I say it I realize I haven't gone since before Gramps died.

"Is that so?" Paul says, looking pleased. "We'll have to go sometime."

"Sounds like a plan," I say, mainly to be cordial—but also aware that I already like him and the idea doesn't sound horrible to me.

Another couple of cousins show up—"on my Dad's side," Haley explains. "This is Lexi, and this is James." James has brought a girlfriend no one has met before, making me feel all the less like the odd man out.

Dinner is surprisingly pleasant—the food is good, lots of people are talking at once, and the game remains on in the other room, adding to the happy cacophony. Paul says he hears I've designed a skyscraper about to be built downtown, and I can tell people are interested, so I share some of the big-picture details, pleased to know I've made a good impression on Haley's dad with my work.

Later, the event becomes more scattered—board games on the dining room table, puzzles in the family room—and though it's long since gotten dark outside, I realize the time's gone quickly and I don't mind that I'm still here. When Paul suggests a game of Monopoly, I announce that I'm in without even considering what a long game it can be. As a group of us sit down around the dining room table, I go so far as to brag that I'm a Monopoly grand champion.

It's a little bit true, but more a habit of bravado in my family—both Grandpa Ed and my dad used to make the same claim. A pleasant memory from my childhood involves standing around a table watching grownups play cutthroat games of Monopoly—of being thrilled when my father would pull me up into his lap so I could feel more like a part of the game.

"A true grand master," Aunt Nan says loudly from where she's drying plates in the kitchen, "has a preferred game piece." Then she laughs. "And it's usually the same one everyone else wants."

As Paul, Hannah, and Cousin Lexi loudly say at the same time, "The car," Haley says, "The cat," and I say, "The wheelbarrow."

Everyone looks at me. "The wheelbarrow?" Hannah questions, like I'm crazy.

But I keep my tough talk going. "I don't need a fancy car to try to intimidate the rest of you—I'm good with simpler transportation."

The line gets a laugh and makes me think of Grandpa Ed, who indeed taught me to enjoy being the wheelbarrow with that same silly claim. "And you never have to feel you lost that first battle," Grandpa once explained, "because nobody else wants to be the wheelbarrow."

Soon enough we're at it, buying up property—it's me, Paul, Hannah, Lexi, and Dan, with little Cora standing by watching. Everyone else is cleaning up the kitchen or finishing a puzzle in the next room, and I've barely even noticed that Haley isn't nearby and I'm having a good time with these people I don't know.

Realizing Cora wants to play but is far too little, I remember that feeling all too keenly and say, "Cora, would you like to be my partner?"

At her eager nod, I can tell both her parents are wondering why *they* didn't think of that.

Cora kneels in a chair next to me in order to be tall enough to see the board, and I make a big deal of consulting her for certain decisions. "What do you think—should we buy Marvin Gardens?"

She shakes her head decidedly no. I already have Atlantic Avenue, so I work to persuade her. "Are you sure, partner? Because the yellow properties are good ones."

She considers it very seriously, our eyes connecting, until she says, "Okay, if you think so."

"Good call," I tell her.

I let her roll the dice when it's my turn and pick cards when I land on Chance or Community Chest.

As the hour grows late, I'm pretty sure we're going to win —but then Paul makes a comeback and buries us all. Before we know it, we're all mortgaging property or selling it to him outright to pay our rent, and I realize *he's* a grand champion and that it would have been fun to watch my grandpa play him.

As we all say goodnight and head out into the chill to our separate cars, Haley smiles up at me and asks, "Was that so bad?"

"No, I had a good time," I'm happy to admit. "Better than I expected."

She squeezes my hand and says, "Thank you for coming. I could tell they all like you."

"I like them, too."

And it hits me that I've spent a whole afternoon and evening with these people without once thinking about my losses. I thought about Gramps, and about my mom and dad —but I didn't think about wishing things were different, or feel like something was missing.

Maybe it's just growing up. Maybe it's the passage of time. Or maybe it's something else that has to do with Haley, and with the people who made her who she is. But I decide not to analyze it too closely and just be glad it was a nice day.

Haley

I love how one day it's Thanksgiving, and it's all fall leaves and pumpkins, and the next morning you wake up and it's suddenly Christmastime. That's how it's always been in *my* family anyway, and how I like it. I want to eke every last bit of fall from the calendar, but the second Thanksgiving is over, I burst into Christmas going ninety miles an hour.

My life is fairly overrun with Christmas trees, but I'm not complaining. I usually help Mom with hers, a live one, and I squeeze one into my apartment—but it has to be the narrow artificial kind due to lack of space. We put one up in the bakery and host a community tree-trimming party on the Saturday after Thanksgiving, inviting customers to bring in an ornament to hang while we all eat Christmas cookies.

This year, my sweet customer Graham surprises Hannah and me both with little holiday gift bags. We open them at the same time to find that mine contains a ceramic ornament shaped like a star, but painted as if it were a cut-out cookie, brownish edges and yellow for the icing, with the year painted in red. Hannah's ornament is a stocking, also painted like a cookie in red and white, and dated.

"These are amazing, Graham!" I gush.

"I painted them myself. Like cookies," he says, to make sure we notice that part.

"I love it!" I tell him. "That's so clever!"

And Hannah says, "Thank you, Graham! That was very thoughtful."

"Everybody is always hanging ornaments on the tree at your party, but you guys don't. Now you both have one to hang up."

See why I love Graham? I give him a hug and tell him what an awesome guy he is.

It's so busy in the shop that I don't even realize Ben has snuck in until he steps up behind me, whispering low in my ear, "You're pretty awesome yourself, bakery lady."

When I turn, his face is so close to mine that I want to kiss him, but it seems out of place in this setting—only I do it anyway because I can't help myself, just a quick but potent kiss that reminds me I'm loving this holiday season even more because I have a boyfriend, and a boyfriend at Christmastime makes it all the more magical.

Yesterday we put up my tree together. And next weekend we're getting a live one for his place. When I found out he hasn't put a tree up since his grandfather died, I insisted. His friend, Terrence, and his girlfriend are going to come over and help. Though I'm pretty sure Terrence just wants to meet me, and that suits me fine. I want to meet him, too.

16

Haley

Two weeks before Christmas I realize I'm having maybe the best holiday season of my life. Romance indeed makes everything merrier. Parties and gatherings, shopping and decorating, plus extra orders at the bakery—add in a boyfriend and I've been kept happily busy.

I indeed met Terrence and Olivia and like them both very much. Although one moment from the tree-trimming party has stayed on my mind. When Terrence and I found ourselves alone, he privately, rather casually, said how glad he was Ben had met me and that, "The guy can be a major commitmentphobe, but maybe that's changing." He ended with a wink that was meant to reassure me.

But it actually did kind of the opposite. It made me wonder: Is Terrence wrong to be so optimistic?

I mean, Ben and I get along great, we have fun, and we agree easily on most things—but there are moments when he pulls back a little, and I'm not sure what that's about. Maybe the losses he's suffered?

And yes, Thanksgiving turned out awesome—everyone loved him, and you'd never have known he wasn't into big family gatherings. And the fact that he originally didn't want to come but then came anyway, and it all went so well, has had me in that happy place.

Only...we've never had a conversation about commitment and I've been nervous to push it. Though what happened with Austin scarred me—when you've found out the guy you're in love with has been dating someone else the whole time, it makes you want to know you're in a solid relationship.

Ben and I haven't talked about that, and we've still never said the 'L' word. I keep wanting to, but I still don't want to be *that* girl: the chaser, the needy one. We've been dating three months now—in some ways a long time, but in others not. Maybe I shouldn't rush him. I've never been accused of being patient, but maybe now is the time to be. He's had a different sort of life than me, with losses I can't begin to understand.

Two weekends before Christmas, he picks me up and we drive down to Covington's Mainstrasse Village Christmas Walk. The area is strong with German roots, and the historic district brims with trendy restaurants and quaint shops.

Bundled in knit hats and warm winter jackets, we walk hand-in-hand—actually mitten-in-glove—past a small park where the Goose Girl fountain is decked out in holiday boughs of green, and a group of costumed carolers stand alongside the Grimm's fairytale character singing *Silent Night*. Across the street sits a jolly Santa on a throne, with teenagers in elf suits managing the queue of kids lined up with their wishlists.

We stroll by shops in 19th century buildings where candles glow in the windows, occasionally stopping in. They all smell deliciously of pine or bayberry or cinnamon—and when we exit back onto the sidewalk after the last to see it's begun to snow, it feels magical.

"Hungry?" Ben asks, and we buy cups of hot cocoa at a kiosk on the edge of the park, along with a bag of roasted almonds and some pumpkin bread to share. We find a bench near the Goose Girl.

All around us, kids run and play, excited about the snow, excited about Christmas.

"Do you want kids someday?" Ben asks.

The question throws me—it's so simple, and yet my mind races, worried I'll give the wrong answer. I mean, I know there's no *wrong* answer, but there is when you hope yours matches the other person's.

I nearly choke on an almond before I manage a reply. "Yeah, I've always hoped to have one or two when the time comes." *And oh my God, I so want that to be with you.* I've never let myself go there until this minute, but it makes me realize all the more how hard I've fallen for him. I totally want to have his babies.

The burst of hidden emotion makes me begin to babble. "I've always loved kids, and I've loved watching my sister become a mom—honestly, I think it's made Hannah a nicer, softer person. I like the idea of parenthood making us better. I mean, I like myself fine, but I also like the notion that bringing forth another life might bring out the best in me, you know? What about you?" Unfortunately, that last part didn't sound casual—it sounded like a woman who's dying to know if our feelings mesh.

He hesitates, torturing me, and finally says, "I think I do."

Again, my mind races. It suddenly feels as if it was a trick question, even if unintentionally, like no answer I could have given would match his. And since I now know I desperately want to have children with him, I suffer the wild need to dig into what his vague, uncertain answer means. Though I try to dig in a cool, casual way. "You're not sure?" I ask as nonchalantly as I can. "You seem great with kids." He charmed my whole family with his attention to Cora at Thanksgiving.

My heart rump-a-pum-pums against my chest as I await his answer—which seems forever in coming. He finally says, "You've probably gathered I don't like talking about what happened to my mom and dad."

"Yeah," I say. He's told me next to nothing about them, in fact. And I've wanted to ask, but it's felt like an off-limits topic.

"When they died," he begins, "it was Christmastime and they were shopping, getting me a bike. I'd been wanting one, but it was a high-priced item for us, so it was a big surprise. Gramps told me later, and the mangled bike was found in the wreckage."

He stops, scrunching up his mouth, looking distant. "I knew it wasn't my fault—but at the same time, you can't help playing that 'what if?' game. Like if I'd never asked for a bike, maybe they wouldn't have been in that exact place at that exact time. Or maybe they would have—who can say? But it still messes with your head when you're a kid."

His words take my breath away. "I can see where it would mess with *anyone's* head, kid or adult," I tell him. "But they're questions without answers. And I'm glad you understand it wasn't your fault." I squeeze his hand.

"Even so, I've still spent a lot of years wishing I'd never asked for that damn thing."

"You can't do that to yourself, Ben."

"I know," he answers, "but I do it anyway sometimes. Because that one moment changed *everything*. Everything about my life. And it ended *theirs*. They were only in their thirties, not much older than I am now."

I nod, taking that in. "I guess it makes Christmas a difficult time for you."

"Gramps tried to make Christmases as special as he could, to help me quit associating it with the loss," he tells me, "but it's always kinda still there."

I find myself circling back to how we got here. "So all of that makes you...not sure you want kids?"

He nods. "Deep down, I do want them. But the idea of having kids holds a little more drama for me than most people. That whole 'what if something happens to me?' question enters in."

I can see where he's coming from, but ... "Let me ask you a question, Ben. Do you think, if your parents had known they'd die young, it would have made them any less eager to have you?"

When he swings his head around to look at me, I can see my point hit home. "No. No, I guess not."

"And personally, I'm so glad they did." *Because I can't imagine my life without you in it suddenly.*

At this, he leans over and kisses me in the snow. It seems like a good answer. And even though I have those niggling concerns about where we are in our relationship, moments like this make it easy to set them aside.

We sit quietly after that, finishing up our wintry snacks in a comfortable silence that adds to my sense of peace. A few minutes later, he asks, "Ready to explore some more?"

"Absolutely," I reply, taking his glove-covered hand in mine.

We've just dropped our cups and wrappers in a trash can and are passing back by the fountain when I hear a familiar voice say, "Hold it right there."

I look up to find Sienna, who I knew would be here photographing the event for the city. She looks sleek and stylish in a fluffy hat and furry zip-up vest. "Hey there!" I say, starting toward her.

But she throws up a hand, abruptly halting both my speech and movement. "I mean it—freeze. This is a great shot."

That's when I realize it's Ben and me with the Goose Girl Fountain on a perfect, snowy night. She raises her camera and instructs us, "Look at each other." So we do. And she snaps, snaps, snaps.

Eventually she says, "At ease," then comes toward us laughing, camera down, hand out. "You're obviously Ben and I'm so happy to finally meet you!"

"And you're obviously Sienna," he greets her with a smile.

I'm grateful he was a good sport about the pictures, and

am also thinking what an amazing memento of tonight they'll be. Maybe I'll frame one as a Christmas gift for him!

"I can't believe we haven't met yet," Sienna goes on. "I feel like I know you, and I look forward to *actually* knowing you." She's still laughing good-naturedly, and I suddenly sense Ben growing a little uncomfortable with her overt friendliness, but I'm not sure why.

Though before I can even examine that, I hear, "Haley Munson, is that you!" And I look over to see my old neighbors.

"Oh my gosh!" I adored them and hated when they moved away. "It's so good to see you guys!" We exchange all the 'how are you?'s before I finally get to introductions. "Mr. and Mrs. Rodriguez, you remember Sienna, and this is my boyfriend, Ben. The Rodriguezes lived next door when I was growing up."

Mr. and Mrs. R. are busy saying hi to Ben and Sienna, and telling me they've been meaning to stop into the bakery because they hear great things, and I'm wrapped up in the conversation, but at the same time...did Ben go a little wooden when I called him my boyfriend? Surely I'm imagining that, yet suddenly his demeanor feels a bit left of center, more rigid. I've introduced him to plenty of people over recent months, but is this the first time I've *called* him my boyfriend? Is it the first time someone close to me has acted so excited to meet him, and as if she expects to be a big part of his life by virtue of our relationship?

Maybe I *am* imagining it, though. Because there's a lot going on suddenly—in fact, it's just as the Rodriguezes move on and Sienna says, "I'd better get back to work, but let's all have dinner soon, okay?" that someone calls Ben's name.

We both turn to see a middle-aged couple approaching, and I gather quickly they both work in his office. The woman, being friendly, informs me, "Ben's cube is right next to mine and he's always nice enough to bring me coffee in the morning."

"That means you're Alicia," I say, pleased to be so in the loop.

"Yes," she says, smiling. "Nice to meet you. And you are?"

Mortified. I'm mortified, and everything inside me stiffens. If I know about Alicia, why doesn't Alicia know about me? If Ben has talked to me about *her*, why hasn't he ever talked to her about *me*? Especially given that we see each other constantly.

Jumping in, Ben says, "Alicia and Todd, this is my friend, Haley."

I hear myself saying, "Nice to meet you," and feel my mittened hand lifting in a hello wave, but my blood has run cold.

Just when I think I know where I stand with Ben, I'm finding out that maybe I know nothing at all. And it feels all too familiar. I thought I knew where things stood with Kirby. And I thought I understood what my relationship was with Austin, as well. But I've learned how wrong I can be. One minute Ben is confiding in me and kissing me and making me feel like the only person on the planet—and the next I'm not even in his universe.

Maybe I've misread *everything*. And I admit it's gotten

more serious for me since we started sleeping together. It's a big thing for me. In my heart, I've never understood how it's not big for everyone—because how do you be that close, that unguarded with someone, without it mattering? But maybe it means as little to Ben as it did to Kirby and Austin.

Or...maybe I'm blowing this out of proportion. Jumping to conclusions. And again, not being patient. Dating is hard. Falling for someone is harder. Oh, the head games we play with ourselves trying to figure it all out.

So I'm going to shake this off and just move on with the evening. We were having such a magical time before this flurry of weird introductions—maybe we can get back to that.

When my phone beeps, I pull it from my pocket to see a text from Mom. *Ask Ben to weigh in on the turkey/ham issue.*

She's been reminding me about this for a week, but I keep forgetting. "Mom wants to know whether you vote turkey or ham for Christmas," I say.

He looks over at me. "What?"

I explain, "It's a big debate in our family. Some people want turkey, but some feel that since we just had turkey for Thanksgiving, we should have ham for Christmas. So every year we take a vote." Then I lean closer and whisper, "And no pressure, but Mom and I are both in the turkey camp." I smile and go on. "The ham always ends up dry for some reason—and I'm pretty sure that reason is my dad thinking he can cook a ham, but he should really just stay out of the kitchen."

"Well," Ben says slowly, seeming to take the question more seriously than makes sense to me, "I guess I like both."

"You still have to vote," I inform him playfully. "It's a family tradition."

When he still hesitates, however, I start getting the same feeling I had when I met Alicia, and the same feeling I had that day in the park when I invited him to Thanksgiving, assuming he'd come. So I find myself rushing ahead, seeking assurances. "We have our Christmas celebration on Christmas Eve," I tell him. "Same basic crowd as Thanksgiving. Then on Christmas Day, Aunt Nan and I usually end up back at Mom and Dad's—we eat leftovers and watch Christmas movies and just hang out. Hannah's family has Christmas with Dan's family that day, so it's a little quieter at the house. You're definitely welcome at both, if you like. Or if you have plans with Terrence, you can come to whichever fits your schedule." I'm rambling at this point. Waiting for him to say that reassuring thing I've been wishing for the whole time.

Finally, though, I shut up. Because I'm out of stuff to say. And so he'll have to say *something*.

What he comes up with is, "Um, Haley...I'm not sure."

"Not sure what? Of your exact plans? Or whether you want to spend Christmas with me at all?" Okay, that was *not* nonchalant. Or graceful. Or gracious.

His brow knits. "It's not that I don't want to see you at Christmas. I just..."

Have no further way to explain apparently, since he drifts off into a silence that both wounds and embarrasses me.

And yes, I want to be graceful. I want to be patient. But I feel like I did that day in the park—I don't want to play games, and I don't want to get any more head-over-heels for him if he really isn't *in* this the way I am.

It would kill me to lose him—but sometimes *patient* and

casual ends up being *mousy* and *walked on.* It's two sides of the same coin, and the only defining factor is how much the other person cares for you.

I drop his hand from mine as I say, "I know asking this question is typically relationship suicide, but what are we, Ben?" I regret the words even as they leave me, but I couldn't stop myself.

"Huh?" he asks. "What do you mean?"

I barrel forward in deepening regret and the deepening inability to shut up. "When you're kissing me, we don't feel like friends. When we're in bed together, we don't feel like friends. When we're spending every evening and weekend together, we don't feel like friends. But to Alicia, I'm your friend. And she doesn't even know I exist? And even though you have no family, you won't spend Christmas with mine?

"I know this has moved kind of fast, but that wasn't my doing alone. I don't see you as a friend. In fact, I love you. There, I said it. I'm in love with you. For better or worse." Oh God. Talk about relationship suicide. Did I really just blurt that out? *I'm in love with you?* I swore to myself I wouldn't say it. What madness has gotten hold of my tongue?

And apparently I'm not done yet. I'm so horrified by what I just said that now I feel the need to bury it a little, under more words. But at the same time, they're *important* words. Impatient, ungrateful, important words. "I guess my point is, if we're just friends—just friends with benefits or something horrid like that—if I've misread this whole thing and you don't see us having a future together, then maybe we should stop seeing each other."

Yes, I really just went that far.

And I think I actually mean it.

Friend? I'm his *friend*? The more I digest that, the more offensive to me it becomes.

And because of that, I'm still not done spilling my guts—it seems I now want him to know every hurt and pain that's been hiding inside me. "You're not the only one who's lost things, you know—people, relationships. The difference is, the people you've lost didn't leave you by choice. But I've had one too many guys walk out of my life, stomping all over my heart on their way out the door, to keep spending time with someone who obviously doesn't feel for me what I feel for him. So...goodnight."

With that, I turn and walk away.

I have no idea where I'm going, though. Ben drove me here. Maybe I can find Sienna.

And what have I just done? I've gone completely off the deep end and dumped him! For calling me his friend.

But maybe that's good—because I don't want to be used if that's all this is. It seemed like so much more.

But then, doesn't it always?

I'm heeding the warning signs this time, paying attention to the red flags. I should have kept my guard up when he was skittish about Thanksgiving—but when it ultimately went so well, I totally immersed myself in the love I feel for him. In the horrible, wonderful, crappy, spectacular, painful love.

I'm barreling through the park, dodging kids and vendors, barely able to see what's right in front of me or where I'm going. I just need to be alone.

Maybe I'll duck into a shop and call Mom. Or Aunt Nan.

No, Hannah. I can't handle the idea of explaining all this to Mom or Aunt Nan right now.

"Haley."

His voice comes from right behind me. But I keep walking.

"I love you, too."

Okay, this stops me. So fast that Ben literally bumps into me from behind.

I turn, into his arms. "You really do?"

He's holding me now, right in the middle of the park. Flurries still flutter around us, and kids are still playing. But all I see is him.

"It's not easy for me," he confesses. "Relationships. Caring. But I do. I swear I do. I'm just not good at...admitting it. Terrence thinks I'm afraid of, you know, getting attached and then losing someone else I care about."

I draw in a breath, blow it back out. I want to be appeased, but I still...need more.

I just don't want to be that girl who's always chasing love. So I say, "Well, maybe I don't want a guy who isn't good at admitting it. Maybe I want—deserve—a guy who *is*. A guy who's *thrilled* to be my boyfriend. And to come to my family's house for Christmas. And to meet my best friend."

He surprises me by saying, "You're right. You're completely right. You're amazing and you deserve everything good."

But...I'm not clear on where we are. "Are you saying I should find someone who can do that? That it isn't you?" I've gone so far down this road now that I want answers—plain, simple, irrefutable ones.

"No," he tells me. "I'm saying I'll do better. I don't want to go back to life without you. Please don't walk away, Haley. I love you. See? I can do better. Let me keep doing better."

All right, that's more what I was looking for.

Suddenly, I can breathe again. Life makes sense again. I don't have to be crushed and heartbroken and emotionally abandoned, after all.

I bite my lip at the heart-poundingness of the moment and whisper, "Okay. I love you, too. And I want us to keep telling each other that. Because it makes me happy. And because...I want somebody who's...all in. Can you be that, Ben? Can you be all in?"

This time there's no hesitation before he says, "Absolutely. I promise. All in. All the way."

Alrighty then, that's better. So I kiss him. And we stand kissing in the snow without a thought to public displays of affection and whether we're for or against them—I, for one, have forgotten where we are and that anything else exists but Ben Page and his amazing eyes and the fact that he loves me and has promised he won't be afraid of it anymore. And that I believe him.

"And by the way," he says when he comes up for air, "turkey."

"Huh?" I murmur, dazed by the kissing, dazed by the love.

"I vote for turkey. And I would love to spend Christmas with your family."

17

Back to the Wedding Box

Haley

You'd think my anxiety would be through the roof watching our dog run around the yard with Aunt Nan's beautiful gift gripped between her cute little teeth, my husband sweating in his dress shirt and tie as he tries to retrieve it, and with so much about our happiness and future feeling on the line in this moment.

Yet, instead, a sense of calm resolve slowly comes over me as the runaway dog gives me a chance to think back to the days of our courtship, to remember a time when Ben was afraid to have kids. A time when he was afraid to commit in general. A time when he was afraid of what new curveballs life might throw at him when he least expected it.

The more I got to know Ben, the more I understood how different our early lives were. Like so many men, he's not one to spill out his fears, or his hurts. But he's aware of them on the inside. And as he began to let me know about them, I became aware, too—I saw his scars, and I learned that some wounds don't really heal and you just learn to live with them and they become a part of you.

Aunt Nan has always said that all any of us really want is to feel understood, and it must be true, because as soon as I started understanding Ben, he began to understand me, too. And then he was all in, just as he promised me that night in the snow.

And so now—*I'm* the one hesitating? *I'm* the one afraid of change and moving forward?

Back then, I understood why Ben was afraid, but I also knew that if he just trusted me, trusted *us*, trusted *life*, that it would all be okay. And I'm guessing that's exactly how Ben feels right now. He wants me to trust him. And trust us. And trust life. And know it's all okay.

I watch as a subtle, coaxing, mental tug-of-war takes place between Ben and Daphne over our now beloved, almost-mythical unopened box—and finally, when Ben has one hand on the gift, the other stroking Daphne's neck, she lets it go. He's smiling softly at her now, cooing, "Good girl. What a good girl."

When he pushes back to his feet, the box in his hands, both he and it look a little disheveled, but still in good shape. The whole episode has released the tension that hung in the air, and as he crosses the backyard toward me, I smile and say, "I feel like dogs running away from us are always bringing us closer together."

He replies only with a gentle grin of his own, and I further point out, "The box looks like it survived the ordeal.

A little rough around the edges, but still almost as pretty as it was on our wedding day."

As he sets it back on the small wooden table between the two Adirondack chairs, he shrugs and says, "Doesn't really matter, though, if we're opening it."

"Maybe we won't," I say. "Maybe we don't have to."

He gives his head a quizzical tilt as he eases down into the chair next to mine. "How do you figure?"

"Let's have a baby, Ben."

He blinks and sits up a little straighter, clearly stunned. "Huh?"

"Let's have a baby. I'm ready."

"Are you sure?" He tilts his head. "Because I don't want to force you into something—"

"I'm sure," I cut him off with a happy nod. "I don't even know why I've been hesitating. Maybe I just needed to wrap my head around the change in timing. But it's what I want, what I've always wanted, with you. So why wait?"

18

Haley and Ben's Four-Year Anniversary

Ben

Terrence and I are sitting in the backyard Adirondack chairs facing downtown Cincinnati on a beautiful June night. He holds up a beer and says, "To the Talcrita Tower officially making it onto the horizon."

After I clink my Blue Moon against his, we both lean back in our chairs and just look. Nearly five years after our building design was chosen, it's finally rising into the skyline high enough to see it taking shape from across the river. Some of that time was spent on planning and permits, after which laying the foundation finally began, and now we're into the faster-moving part of construction.

Though we've been working on other projects, we still visit the job site regularly. And it's beyond fulfilling to see the dream becoming a reality from my own backyard. Another year, give or take, and it'll be the skyline's newest gem, visible for miles.

"We did it," Terrence says.

"Indeed we did."

Again, we both go a little quiet—maybe we're in awe. Maybe we're both putting the years, the achievement, in perspective.

"I feel so much older now than when we designed it," I muse.

He takes a sip from his bottle. "We've both done a lot of living since then."

Terrence is married now, too—and after tying the knot last fall, they're already expecting their first child. We've gone only from our twenties into our early thirties during the whole process, but in some ways it feel like we've grown from boys into men.

"Not a bad way to mark time, though," he adds, sounding satisfied. "We keep going, and by the time we're old, we'll have added a lot to this city that'll be here long after we're gone."

I just nod, the idea not new to me. It's probably why I'm an architect—wanting to create things that'll outlast me, things I'll never have to lose.

"Speaking of marking time," he says, "didn't you and Haley just have an anniversary? What is it, now? Four?"

Another nod from me as I take a drink. "Yep." But I leave it at that.

And he notices. "Um, there's nothing wrong there? Between you and Haley?"

I look over and quickly reassure him, "Of course not. She's great."

"Then what's wrong? Because for a man with a beautiful

wife, a beautiful home, and a great career, you haven't seemed...exactly on top of the world lately."

I shrug. "When you put it like that, I feel like a jerk. I should be happy, right?"

He returns the shrug. "Right. But why aren't you? What's up, man?"

This has been going on for months, but I haven't wanted to talk about it. Guess I should fill him in, though. "We can't have a baby."

I'm still looking out at the city as I say it, but in my peripheral vision I sense him pulling back in shock. "Damn," he murmurs. "I didn't see that coming. Though...I was kinda wondering. I knew you guys were trying. What's the deal?"

I blow out a breath, pushing myself to have the conversation. It's not that I mind him knowing—it's that saying it out loud makes it all the more a reality I can't shove under the rug and ignore. "We tried casually for a while, and it didn't happen. Then we tried in a more serious way—the whole take-the-temperature and be-at-the-ready-when-the-conditions-are-right thing. And it still didn't work. So we had some tests done."

"And?" he asks.

I release another tired breath. "Without getting into technicalities, we both have issues that make it a lot harder to get pregnant. The doctor said if we only had one thing going against us, we might still have a shot at it—but that all the contributing factors add up to it being highly unlikely we'll ever conceive. Like a one percent chance."

I see his brain working—give Terrence a problem and it's his instinct to find a solution in some logical or mathematical way. "So does that mean if you have sex a hundred times, you'll get pregnant on the one-hundredth?"

I shake my head. "Nope, or we'd probably be pregnant by now. It's more like each time, you have that one percent chance. And the doctor hasn't been encouraging—her only advice is to consider alternate means."

"In vitro?" Terrence asks.

Another nod from me.

"And?"

"We decided against it. It was a hard decision, but it's so expensive, and still has a limited chance of working—and there are so many ups and downs of getting through the whole process. We didn't feel good about it."

"I can understand that," he says, then moves on to the next obvious suggestion. "Adoption?"

Though the very word darkens my mood, it's not his fault. It's no one's fault. "Haley wants to adopt, but I don't."

"I'm not surprised."

This draws my glance—I *am* surprised, that he's not. "No?"

"That whole family line thing is important to you."

Oh. Yeah. I probably *did* tell him about that at some point. "Do you think I'm wrong? For feeling that way?"

He shrugs. "You feel how you feel, man. When it comes to something as big as this, it's valid."

Hmm. I thought he'd argue with me. So I say, "Thanks, man."

"Is that okay with Haley, though?"

I shake my head. "No. We're...struggling a little right now. It's a pretty big thing to disagree on."

Haley

"I have a great life, right?" I ask Hannah behind the bakery counter. It's late in the day, the place is mostly quiet, and I'm trying not to feel empty at the thought of never having a child.

"Of course you do," she assures me, wiping her hands on her pink apron. She's mixing icing for someone's wedding cake. "Great husband, great house, *fabulous* sister"—she stops to strike a pose—"two goofy furballs you love, and you run an adorable bakery."

While my whole family has heard the news that Ben and I can't conceive, so far I've only told Hannah the part about him being unwilling to adopt. "And I can have a perfectly full life without kids, right?"

"Right," she says supportively. "And you can borrow mine any time you like." She adds a wink. Cora is ten now and Cole six. I adore them both and Cora is reaching a really fun age where she likes me to do her hair and help her pick out clothes. Maybe being an aunt is the closest I'll ever get to being a mom.

A thought which, contrary to what I was going for, kind of buries me.

As the bell on the door announces rings, Hannah gives my arm a bolstering squeeze, whispering, "It'll be okay," in a big-sister way that would have made me believe when I was twelve, but it's harder now.

I look up as Graham and his mom approach the counter. "Hey, you two." I force a smile. "What can I get you today?"

Graham studies the glass-front counter and points to a thick, walnut-topped brownie.

"Excellent choice," I respond. I tell him that no matter what he picks—though I make mental notes about what he returns to repeatedly because the kid has good taste.

As I ring up the purchase, Graham says, "You look sad, Haley. What's wrong?"

So much for my pasted-on smile. I feel like I'm struggling to even breathe as I say, "Just having a bad day, I guess. But I'll be fine."

"I hope you feel better."

"That goes for both of us," his mom says. I meet her eyes with gratitude, imagining what some of her own struggles might be, and I feel guilty for my sadness. I *do* have a great life. I just wanted a child to be a part of it.

Despite myself, there's a lump in my throat as they leave and a group of teenage girls walks in. While only twenty-nine, I suffer the odd pang of knowing I'll never have a teenage daughter myself.

"Why don't you take a break, step outside for some air," Hannah suggests, coming up beside me. "I'll handle the counter." My sister is good at reading me.

I don't say anything, not even thanks—I just go, not wanting to dissolve in front of customers. I make a beeline for the front door.

I ease into one of the chairs at the table on the sidewalk and bend my head over into my hands. I'm still in public, but too bad—it's a moment of surrender.

"Haley? Honey, what on earth is wrong?"

Surprised to hear a voice I'd know anywhere, I look up to

see Aunt Nan in a flowy lavender top and summer-white capri pants.

"What are you doing here?" I know my cheeks are tear-stained.

"I was just in the neighborhood. What's wrong, honey? Come walk with me."

Aunt Nan always says walking is better than sulking. She believes you get farther—not just geographically but mentally—when you're walking than when you're sitting. I stand up and she locks her arm through mine as we begin strolling up the street.

"All right now," she says as we pass by DeGregorio's, "what on earth has you so upset?"

"Well, you know the news we got from the doctor."

She nods solemnly. "I know how hard news like that is." She does know, better than anyone else in my life; she's been where I am. Which makes her the perfect person to talk to about this. "So that's what this is about?"

As we turn onto a residential street, both sides lined with well-kept English Tudors, I tell her, "Sort of. But it's also that...Ben doesn't want to adopt."

I wait for her to take my side, act like that's crazy. Instead, though, she only asks, "Do you know why?"

"It's complicated," I say. "He feels it's too long of a process, with too many hoops to jump through that still might lead to failure, just like the in vitro. But it also has to do with his family, his grandpa—all that."

"I see." Aunt Nan knows about Ben's past.

"It's something about him I understand," I go on, "but don't think should rule our lives. He's not willing to find the happiness of parenthood in another way—it has to be the way he planned or not at all."

She says to me in a measured tone, "Many people who can't conceive feel that way."

And I wonder something I've never even thought about before. "Did *you* ever consider adopting?" Even now, I'm flummoxed by how well you can know an older family member still without knowing key details of their lives. How have I never asked her this?

She shakes her head. "It seemed complicated, pressure-filled. Philip and I both agreed that we'd just love our nieces extra hard and that would be enough."

The sentiment sinks deep into my heart. It's somehow incredibly sweet and unbearably sad at the same time. "Was it?" I ask. "Enough? It's okay if you want to say no."

She looks over and smiles her Aunt Nan smile. Her face is so close to mine that I see her eyes more clearly than usual —a pale, flecked, watery blue—and I feel in that moment like I'm seeing her very soul. Not just my aunt, but a woman. A woman who knew heartbreak and made hard decisions—and never once let it show to me or Hannah. "The truth is," she tells me, "it's apples and oranges. But I've probably loved you more for not having children of my own."

I bite my lip, feeling emotional. Thinking about pathways and choices. I never realized how I benefited from her loss without ever knowing, even as it was right in front of me. "I'm sure *I've* loved *you* more because of that," I say, "and *felt* your love more, too."

"See?" she says. As if I should know what she means. But

with Aunt Nan, I seldom do until it's spelled out. I sometimes tend to think her a bit dotty or pedestrian—only to later be reminded she possesses a certain profound wisdom located on a slightly different plane than the one where my own brain exists.

"See what?" I ask. Maybe in the past I've asked such questions incredulously, like she's silly or a little foolish—but now I ask with utter sincerity, eager to find out what I'm missing.

"Things unfold as they're meant to," she tells me. "Life can be a complicated journey, and we mere mortals don't always understand all the whys and the hows. And sometimes it even makes us angry—but things do happen as they should. We have to trust in that."

"Only sometimes really *bad* things happen," I argue. "Like Ben's parents getting killed."

"I know it can be hard to accept things that are so painful, so against the plan—that it can seem very wrong. Believe me, that's how I felt when your Uncle Philip died before reaching old age. But after some time I realized that it was just another curve on the journey." She pats my hand, still hooked through her arm, adding, "Though Ben's path has been more difficult than many, I grant you. That's why he's so lucky to have you bringing him the love and joy he never got enough of before losing his family."

Frankly, I've always felt that way, too. However, I don't resist the urge to say, "I'm not feeling too joyful right now." If my purpose is to make Ben's life happy, at the moment it's not working. And doesn't my own happiness matter? In fact, if I hadn't looked out for my own happiness back when we were dating, it's possible the big lug would never have figured out how much he needed me.

"First things first," Aunt Nan says. "Don't lose your faith in life. Don't forget how much you have to be grateful for."

"You're right, I do. I've been reminding myself that."

"Good," she says. "Now, second—be understanding of Ben's needs. And I'm sure he'll be understanding of yours, too. You two occasionally meet up with conflict, but you always find solutions."

I start to argue that. "Except—"

But she holds up her free hand to quiet me, saying, "I know—right now you don't see any possible solution. But that's okay—solutions can grow from the seeds of love."

"Oh," I murmur, "I like that." There were times I would have considered such words pretty yet meaningless—but now I trust her wisdom and take her more seriously.

"Third," she continues, "remember that miracles happen every day. They're all around us. In fact, there are a million miracles around us right now."

Okay, it's not that I don't believe in miracles—but despite my belief in *her*, this particular pretty claim draws some skepticism from me. "Well, if there are so many miracles around, I wish one of them would make me pregnant."

"The ones I'm talking about," she answers without missing a beat, "are already busy bringing about other things you see right in front of you."

This is when I realize she's speaking literally, about the miracles.

"The sky is a lovely shade of blue—that's a miracle to me. When it rains, we see beautiful arcs of light across the sky—

rainbows. If that's not miraculous, I don't know what is. Cars, televisions, airplanes, cell phones, computers—each and every one of those are wild miracles that we've all just gotten used to and have stopped seeing, stopped feeling. We've stopped feeling the miraculousness. Men go to the moon. We send rockets to Mars. And then there are butterflies and flowers and trees—each unique and beautiful." She motions around us on the home-lined street, which indeed boasts trees and flowerbeds all brimming with colorful little...miracles.

"The fact that our bodies heal themselves of so many things," she goes on. "The fact that we breathe without thinking, that our hearts beat the same way. Miracles, miracles, miracles. All we have to do is see them, stay aware of them and remember they happen all the time, and then just be open to getting the ones we want most."

Okay, wow. We humans *are* woefully good at taking miracles for granted. I feel newly in awe of her.

But at the same time, I can't deny still being selfishly stuck on wanting a baby. "And if that never happens?"

She shrugs easily. "It's still a beautiful world, and a beautiful life, filled with more miracles than there are stars in the sky. No matter what happens, you and Ben have a beautiful love and a wonderful existence together—don't forget that. The two of you have so many miracles already."

I take that in. Even our meeting seemed miraculous in a way. It all has, every aspect of our relationship, the good and the bad, the easy and the hard. Maybe I'm beginning to see what she's saying, at least a little. And I also have to acknowledge that, "Some of our bigger miracles have seemed to come directly through you, in one way or another."

She waves a dismissive hand down through the air. "If it seems that way, it's only because I'm open to the miraculous."

She walks me back to the bakery, imparting still more wisdom and assuring me that Ben and I will be okay. And I believe that. I do. But my heart still hurts.

It still hurts, and yet...I also feel uplifted underneath it all. Like I *want* to believe in her miracles. Even if I'm not quite there yet.

When we reach the bakery's pink-and-black-striped awning, Aunt Nan gives me a tight hug and says, "I love you very much, Haley."

"I love you, too," I tell her.

And as she walks away, it occurs to me that we don't say that enough. My family is filled with love, but we show it more than say it. And I'm glad Aunt Nan and I said it today.

Ben

It's been a long few days. Honestly, in some ways, it's been a long year. I've always assumed parenthood would hold challenges, but I thought the act of *making* a baby would be easy. The last few days, disagreeing with Haley on where to go from here has been hard—for both of us. Before leaving downtown after work, I stop at a flower shop near my office and buy a bouquet of daisies.

When I walk in the front door, the dog clamors at my feet, trying to trip me as usual, but I only have eyes for my wife—whose face lights up when she sees the flowers. Her silent response is to hold up a small bakery bag and give me a soft smile. She doesn't need to say what's inside. Daisies and jelly donuts have been our love language from the start.

"I don't want to fight anymore, babe," I say as I reach her, holding out the bouquet.

She accepts them, her expression sweet—and undeniably tired-looking as well. "Me, neither."

"And I don't want to make you unhappy."

"I know. I don't want to make you that way, either."

"We both feel how we feel." The daisies and the donuts lay on the counter now, so I take her hand, rubbing my thumb across the back of it. I love her madly and just want to find a way through this to the other side. "I don't know how to change that, how to make us both happy here. And I don't think even Aunt Nan can fix this one."

She nods. "I saw her today, and we talked."

I tilt my head. "She didn't, did she?" I ask with both skepticism and an ounce of hope. "Magically fix it?" There's a tiny part of me waiting to hear the solution, the thing Aunt Nan said to lead us to the answer.

But Haley shakes her head. "Nope. Guess we finally found the one thing she can't solve. She reminded me, though, that regardless, we're going to have an amazing life together."

"That's an awesome point."

She bites her lip. "Even so, though, I feel like this is...well, a major disagreement. I want a baby however we can get one. And you'd rather be childless than open your heart to an alternative plan."

I try not to bristle as I calmly say, "You're making me sound unreasonable."

She lets out a sigh. "I didn't mean to—I promise. I know you have your reasons, and your feelings are valid. I just worry that later in life you might wish you'd made a different choice. And I want a family with you. Not that I think we can't be happy without one—but I just really *want* one. A year ago you felt the same."

A slight lump forms in my throat. I'm not a guy who cries, but damn—her last line catapults me back in time to a place where that part of life sounded free and easy, like all we had to do was hop into bed birth-control-free and nature would take its course. Life felt so much more carefree then. Okay—maybe no one would describe me as a carefree guy—but compared to now, I *was* those things. Now something in my heart has hardened. Maybe I'm mourning the son we'll never have.

I take a deep breath, try to shove the emotion away, and state my case. I've stated it before—but this is the calmest conversation we've had about it, so possibly it's worth saying again, in case she hears it differently this time. "A year ago, I wanted us to have a baby. But if we can't have one, I don't want us to kill ourselves working our way through a system that might leave us disappointed, or even more heartbroken. I just feel like...if we were meant to have a kid, we'd have it."

She doesn't answer right away—I sense her doing the same thing I am, trying to stay kind, not let this escalate. We're both trying so hard.

Just then, her phone rings, but she silences it, setting it back on the kitchen counter, clearly in no mood to take a call.

Finally, she says, "I think we should open the box."

"Don't think it hasn't crossed my mind," I say. "Only...

we've started opening the box so many times before, but something always stops us—something that ultimately means we don't need to open the box."

"Isn't that a good enough reason?" she asks, eyebrows lifting.

I see her point, yet... "I'm just saying that whatever's in there isn't gonna fix this. There's no magical solution. And if we decide to open it, I don't think anything's gonna stop us this time. So it'll...really be open. No closing it back up." Part of me hates the mythic proportions the box has taken on, but I just want her to be sure.

She seems pretty resolute, though, when she says, "Aunt Nan never meant it to be something we held onto for this long. And I know it won't fix anything, but if whatever is in that box makes us feel a little better about disagreeing on something so huge, then now's the time."

I nod in agreement. "Okay. You're right."

"Would you mind getting it," she asks, "while I put these in water?" She motions toward the daisies. "I don't want them to wilt."

I don't want us *to wilt.* That's what I'm thinking as I climb the stairs to the spare bedroom closet where Aunt Nan's wedding gift now resides. I pull it down from a shelf, knowing what Haley said is true—Aunt Nan never meant for us to wait this long. It's time to find out what's in the box at last. It just stinks knowing that when we're through, we'll still have this enormous problem standing between us.

Even so, as I descend the stairs, gift in hand, I can't deny growing eager to finally see what's inside. I find my wife still fiddling with the daisies—cutting the stems into the sink, lowering them into a water-filled vase and fluffing them a little.

"Ready to do this?" I ask with a smile. It's almost a real smile. Because of the anticipation. And because what Aunt Nan said today is true—we'll always be happy. Okay, true, I'm wondering how that can happen if one of us doesn't get our way on the biggest thing we could possibly not see eye to eye on—but I'm trying to push that aside.

"Yes," she says—and when she comes toward the kitchen table, where I've placed the gift, I see all those same warring emotions reflected in her eyes.

"Go ahead," I tell her. "Unwrap it."

19

Before...

Ben

It's a cold, snow-covered day in February, and Terrence copped out of running, so I came to the cemetery instead. Just driving through the gates makes me remember that first crazy day I met Haley here—the great dog chase. The memory makes me realize I probably haven't been here since she and I started dating back in September, so I feel a little guilty—but I think Gramps would like that I've been keeping so busy with a girl I love.

We have the perfect kind of snow right now—eight inches fell a few days ago, but we've had sunny days since, clearing and drying the roads. So it's pretty in that wintry way, but easy to get around. I park just inside the gates, pull a knit hat on with my sweats, and run along the twisting drive that leads to Grandpa Ed's grave.

The run naturally winds past Haley's uncle's resting place and I see that she and Aunt Nan have dutifully decked it out for Valentine's Day—red silk roses in the vases, and in the bare tree limbs above, red and pink bows are accompanied by a few little heart ornaments. All the decorations are laced with snow.

As I approach Gramps, I notice red silk roses in his vase, too. Which I didn't put there. I glance over my shoulder to the other headstone, and my heart swells to realize Haley's been putting flowers on my grandfather's grave, too, without even telling me.

I stop when I get there, looking down on his name and the dates that mark his life. I wonder if you ever stop feeling it—the strangeness that the person you love is no longer here. I hardly ever visit my parents' graves in the country—I feel guilty about that, too, but my last thought is the reason: having to refresh that feeling of *the void*, that feeling of *why?*, that feeling of how can someone be here one minute and just *gone* the next. Where is it that they go?

"I should take Haley down to Mom and Dad's graves one day," I say out loud. "She'll be happy to go with me. Heck—she'll bring flowers for the vases." I end on a little laugh. I'd like to believe I'm just talking to myself, but given where I'm standing, I know I'm doing that thing I don't think makes any sense but which became our family tradition—talking to a grave.

"So, if I'm here talking to you, I might as well just go there—be all in, right? Like Haley said about us—her and me—back in December."

Reminiscing about that brings a smile. "I have been ever since, by the way," I say. "Haley is the girl I'm dating. I wish you could meet her." I never gave that a thought with Taryn.

"You'd love her. She's the one who brought you the flowers. That's how sweet she is. And even though I was crazy about her, I kept having this knee-jerk reaction about moving the relationship forward." I stop, blink, flinch a little. I know it was all because of my family dying on me, and the reason I'm flinching is because I don't like admitting I'm so...predictable.

"Anyway," I go on in a low voice, "she was about to walk away because I was hesitating. And it hit me like a ton of bricks: What the hell is it I'm running from? When I should probably be running *to* it. Because she's probably the best thing that's ever happened to me. So I told her I loved her—because I do. And ever since, things are great. Her family is awesome—I wish you could meet them, too. You wouldn't even mind having Thanksgiving with them." I add a laugh, and for a brief second, it's like he's really here with me.

I wasn't sure why I came here today other than realizing I haven't in a while—but maybe I just needed to tell my grandfather about Haley. Even as much as I don't believe a dead man is at his grave, this is as close as I can come to finding him somewhere.

I continue my run through the cemetery and, with the sun blasting down, I actually find the cold invigorating and the mantle of snow beautiful. Still running, I pull out my phone and text Haley. I've told her I'm planning something special for Valentine's Day—but now I'm formulating a different idea. So I'll let her decide.

Hey babe! For Valentine's Day, it's choose your own adventure. Option 1: Fancy dinner at undisclosed but pricy downtown hot spot. Option 2: Winter Fun Day.

A few minutes later my phone buzzes, and I happily

check her reply, even though I'm pretty sure I know what she picked.

I'm not sure what a Winter Fun Day is comprised of, but I'm in!

Just like I thought. She'd rather have fun in a winter coat and hat than be wined and dined. The nouveau riche city slicker in me would have chosen the dinner for this particularly auspicious occasion—and good old Taryn would have chosen the dinner twenty times over, too. But the real me—the guy who came and conquered but inside is still the same person he always was—is happy with Haley's choice. Winter Fun Day, here we come.

Haley

Is there anything better than being in love? Okay, well, let me rephrase. Is there anything better than being in love with someone who's just as in love with you? Because I've been in love before—but never like this.

Part of me is still amazed. When I came unraveled at the Christmas Walk, tossing out maniacally unplanned ultimatums, I did *not* see things going my way. But later, Ben told me it woke him up, and that he'd hated knowing he'd hurt me. I would never recommend going the maniac-ultimatum route, but I guess once in a blue moon *anything* works. Law of averages. If a hundred girls gave a hundred ultimatums, ninety-nine of them would probably backfire—but I was the lucky one whose guy saw past the lunacy to the love underneath.

Now it's Valentine's Day and we've both taken off work for Winter Fun Day. We start with sledding on the hill in front of the band shell at Devou Park. "This brings back memories," I tell him when we arrive at this first surprise location. "My dad used to bring Hannah and me here on snow days when we were little." Although neither of us can remember the last time we went sledding, Ben borrowed two sleds from Terrence for the occasion, and it's fun doing something together that makes me feel like a kid again.

After that, he drives us to Mt. Adams, a trendy, historic neighborhood on a high peak just east of downtown, where we warm up with lunch at a cute, cozy restaurant. From there, we head into adjacent Eden Park, the oldest in the city, and Ben parks near Mirror Lake, a shallow manmade body of water that erupts with fountains in the summertime but in the winter makes the perfect ice-skating rink. Besides skaters, there are kids playing in the snow and people walking dogs.

We rent ice-skates in the large, historic gazebo that has overlooked the lake for over a hundred years. Same as with the sledding, neither of us have ice-skated since we were kids, so we're both pretty wobbly, but we hold hands as we ease out onto the ice, laughing.

"Come on, Munson," he says, "give me a triple axel!"

I tell him, "I'll be lucky if I don't *land* on my axel."

"Yeah, this seemed easier when I was ten," he agrees.

"Where did you skate as a child?"

"On the pond beside our farmhouse," he replies with a smile. "My parents got me skates for Christmas when I was eight, and Dad taught me that winter." It's the happiest I've ever seen him when talking about his parents.

We make our way around the lake with other skaters, many as unsteady as us while others glide along so smoothly they probably *could* pull off an Olympic-style jump or two. Eventually, we both move a little more comfortably and it even becomes fun.

Until I do land on my axel—with a thump. Ben comes skating to my rescue. "Oh, that's gonna cost her with the judges," he says playfully, taking my hands to help me up. "You okay?"

"Yep," I assure him. "Just got too confident and tried a turn I shouldn't have."

"Here, let's hold hands again," he suggests, and there's no denying I feel more secure with his hand in mine.

And as we glide across the ice, it hits me that I've started to depend on that—the security of his hand in mine, even just metaphorically. We say 'I love you' all the time now. But we haven't talked much about our future, and in this moment I pray he doesn't decide to let go of my hand in the big-picture way.

I recently told Aunt Nan that sometimes it scares me how in love with him I am. She said, "Love is always a risk. Always. But it's worth it."

"Are you saying love always works out?" It was one of those times when I felt like I wasn't quite keeping up with her.

But she shook her head and said, "No, dear. I'm saying if you don't take the risk, you never know love. And that's the greatest shame of all—for anyone."

I let that hearten me now, choosing to focus on the fact that it's Valentine's Day and Winter Fun Day and I'm with the guy I adore.

When we've had enough skating, we change back into

our snow boots, turn our skates in, and sit on a bench, watching two little boys throw snowballs at each other. They look to be around six and eight years old, and they're with a lady on a bench near ours, probably their grandmother. Soon one of them says, "Let's make a snowman."

Ben is watching the kids intently, so much so that I ask, "What's on your mind?"

"Thinking about my grandpa," he says. "About some stuff he said to me when he was dying."

Whoa. Nothing heavy about that. I blow out a breath. But I love when he confides in me, so I ask, "What did he say?"

Ben lets out a sigh. "He was still sad about the loss of his family, of his only son."

"Your dad."

Ben nods. "All those years later, and I guess he'd never made peace with it."

"They say there's nothing harder than losing a child," I reply. Though I'm not sure Ben has ever made peace with it, either. And I can't fault him for that, but my heart longs to help him try.

"This is super old-fashioned, I guess, but he talked about wanting his bloodline to go on," Ben tells me. "He said he'd been proud of my dad and was proud of me, too, for all I've accomplished so far, and that he took peace in knowing someday I'll have a son. He said he worked hard his whole life, like his father before him, and that seeing me succeed made it worthwhile. And that when I have a son someday, he wants me to tell him family stories, and show him pictures, so he'll know where he came from."

I stay quiet, taking all that in. I guess impending death makes you yearn to keep existing in some way, even if only through future generations. And of course my chest aches with wanting those children to be mine, but I push that down so I won't feel desperate on Winter Fun Day. Thus I come back to, "There are family pictures?"

He glances over, nodding. "I have some old photo albums in storage."

I gasp softly, a little horrified. "I think your grandpa would want them out. More accessible."

"You're right. I just...haven't looked at them in a really long time. You know?"

Yeah, I know. One more confirmation of his never having gotten past his parents' deaths. "Will you show them to me?" I ask. "I'd really like to see your family."

He doesn't respond right away, but after a moment replies, "Yeah, okay. In fact..."

"Yes?"

"I was thinking about asking you to drive down to their graves with me, and maybe I can show you where Gramps and I lived, and the house where I lived with Mom and Dad before that. If you want."

"Of course I want. I'd love to see where you grew up."

"Oh—and thank you. For the flowers on Grandpa Ed's grave." He leans over and kisses me.

"If I knew it was going to get me kisses," I say with a flirtatious grin, "I'd have told you."

Our eyes lock in a way that makes me feel less worried he'll let go of my hand.

Our romantic gaze is interrupted, however, by one of the little boys yelling at the other. "You're not doing it right!"

The other boy responds with, "This is stupid! Why's it gotta be so hard?"

We both swing our gazes in their direction. "Snowman problems," I observe quietly. They've moved a lot of snow around the last few minutes, but so far there's nothing remotely resembling even the base of a snowman.

"I should probably lend my architectural expertise to the situation," Ben announces, then stands up and approaches the kids. "Hey guys, don't get frustrated. Snowman construction can take a little practice. Want some help?"

They exchange glances and the older one says, "Okay."

Then Ben tosses a look to their grandma. "Is it okay if I give these guys a few snowman pointers?"

The woman smiles her thanks. "Absolutely. Before they kill each other."

I'm again taken by how adorable Ben is with children, and I love watching him help the two little guys make a snowman. Of course, it's mostly Ben doing the work, but he's sly enough to convince them they're the ones making it happen.

"Does this seem like a good size for the head?" Ben asks the smaller kid, motioning to a ball of snow he's packed together on the ground.

The kid say, "A little bigger."

Ben pulls back, surveys the snowball. "You're right. Good call. Come help me pack some more snow onto it." Both kids do, using a technique Ben has taught them. Finally, he says to the younger one, "I'm gonna pick you up so you put it in place, okay? Be careful or we'll have to make a whole new head."

After head placement commences a search for suitable sticks and rocks for arms and a face.

"Hey, look what I found!" the older boy says. He's comes back from his search dragging a tattered old green winter scarf someone lost or abandoned long ago. "Perfect!" Ben declares. "What a great find! Good job, buddy!"

When the masterpiece is complete, the boys' grandmother wants a photo, so I take one, too. I post it on social media with the caption: *@BenjaminPage and friends construct the perfect snowman in Eden Park. That architecture degree is really paying off!*

By the time we say goodbye to the kids, we're freezing—the afternoon has grown late and the sun's beginning to set. "I loved our Winter Fun Day," I tell him as we reach the car.

"Well, that's good because we're not done yet."

I raise my eyebrows at him over the car's roof. "No?"

"Get in," he replies.

He blasts the heat on high, getting us pretty toasty again by the time we park on a steep street outside the Blind Lemon, a trendy little hole-in-the-wall bar I've always meant to visit, but never have. I can't deny Ben makes me see our city through fresh eyes.

Entering the bar is a matter of descending narrow, uneven, cave-like steps contained between tight stone walls, until they open into an outdoor patio with multiple fire pits. The space is strung with lights and walled on both sides with old brick—a sunken oasis hidden in the heart of the city. A guitar player sings the Beatles' "In My Life" as we sit down at a café table next to a stone hearth.

Ben suggests hot brandy Alexanders, which I've never had before, but the chocolatey-tasting concoction is delicious. As we sit holding hands, soaking up the warmth of the fire and the drinks, listening to the music, I can't think of anyplace I'd rather be.

An hour later, it's gotten dark and Ben leans over to say, "I have one more stop planned for our Valentine's Day."

I raise my eyebrows in surprise because, seriously, I thought this was it. And honestly, I'm a little tired—it's been an action-packed excursion and I expect to be sore tomorrow from sledding and skating. "Where?" I ask.

"Have you ever been to the overlook behind the Immaculata Church?"

"Is that the one they call the Church of the Steps?"

He nods. Every Easter faithful parishioners stop and pray on each of the dozens of steps that lead up a steep incline to the church, and it's always on the local news. "It's the big stone church you can see from across the river."

"Ohhh," I say, knowing exactly which one he means and feeling both ignorant and enlightened at once. One more instance of not knowing my own city very well. It sits like a majestic beacon on a high peak overlooking the city.

Back in the car, we make turns on narrow streets, and soon enough we find the big stone church towering over us as Ben parks. But only when we reach the overlook do I realize how stunning the view is. "Wow," I say. As I take in downtown Cincinnati from the east, the skyline becomes entirely reorganized. The vista also provides a breathtaking view of the winding Ohio River below, and the expanse of riverfront communities on the other side.

"How do you know all these places?" I ask. "How did you find them?"

He shrugs. "Terrence and I drove around a lot in college. I wanted to learn the city."

"That shouldn't surprise me," I tell him. "You have such a love for it. I feel bad that I take it for granted."

He gives me a grin. "When I take you to the country, you'll probably be charmed by every barn and cow and hillside that *I've* always taken for granted. We're always fascinated by what's new to us."

I take that in, our eyes connecting. And I measure my words carefully as I reply, "Sometimes, though, the new doesn't wear off." Because I don't think the new of Ben will ever start feeling old to me.

He says, "No, sometimes it doesn't. That's the best kind of new."

I think he knows exactly what I'm talking about, and I think he's saying we're on the same page, but I still feel bashful as a blush warms my cheeks despite the cold, so I shift to refocus on the lovely view. "This makes me see the city in a whole new way," I tell him. All the same buildings are there, but from this angle, they're all in different places. "It takes something I thought I knew and rearranges it."

"Maybe that's why I wanted to show it to you," he says. "Because *you* make *me* see things in a whole new way."

It's then that I turn to look at him—and find him down on one knee. He's holding out an open ring box, the diamond inside glittering beneath streetlights.

A gasp leaves me, my heart swelling with a profound mix of shock and joy. Less than a minute ago I was still questioning if he felt as much for me as I do for him. And now the miracle I've been waiting for is really happening! Because love *is* a *miracle*.

"You've changed something in me, Haley. You've made me a better man. And I know there were times I made you doubt me, times when I doubted my own ability to be the man you need. But now there's no more doubt. I know we can make each other happy, come what may. And that it's a new that'll never wear off. Will you marry me?"

"Yes!" I say without reservation. "Yes, yes, yes!"

20

Back to the Wedding Box

Haley

I find myself thinking back to another box I once shared with Ben—one that held my engagement ring. And on the day he proposed, he clearly stated that it was important to him to have a child who bore his grandfather's genes. More and more, I realize that we've *always* been clear with each other about the things that matter to us, but maybe it's easy to not always *hear*. Aunt Nan's wisdom comes back to me: Love makes you blind. Maybe deaf, too, sometimes.

But be all that as it may, this huge disagreement persists. Even if I *was* warned how he felt about it, a couple doesn't sit around thinking they won't be able to have a baby, or deciding what to do if that happens. You don't find out you disagree on *that* until you're *there*.

So this time we're really opening the box. I exchange glances with him, and reverently, I pull the lace ribbon we retied after the last near miss—just as my phone rings.

Sheesh—this is the third call I've had to silence in ten minutes. As I grab the phone to do it again, a glance at the screen shows me it's Mom. Who's usually more patient.

And something about that, no matter how crappy the timing, makes me answer. "Mom?" I say, rather impatiently myself. "What's up? Why all the calls?"

"Honey, are you sitting down?" Her voice is strained. And a cold dread fills my heart.

"Yes. What's wrong?"

"There's no easy way to say this. Honey, your Aunt Nan has died."

21

Three Months Later

Haley

Aunt Nan always said cemeteries are full of stories. It was one of those fanciful-sounding comments that would roll melodiously off her tongue, and that I never paid much attention to. But now that's changed. Now I see the stories.

September has brought gentler air and changing colors after a long, hot summer of loss and mourning, and today, after decking out my aunt and uncle's graves for autumn, I'm walking through the cemetery, remembering that every person here had a story.

The saddest stories, to me, are in the children's section. I see how parents have tried to commemorate their child with teddy-bear-shaped grave markers, engravings of Winnie-the-Pooh, or balloons or lambs or bunnies—one is elaborately carved with the image a little boy holding a fishing pole next to a pond. People leave toy animals, brightly-colored pinwheels, Mylar balloons.

My heart breaks for them and I can only let my heart wander so far into those particular stories. Maybe it hurts a little more knowing I'll never have a child of my own. Perhaps it should instead make me feel protected, safe from ever knowing that particular pain, but it doesn't.

Moving beyond the children's section, every single gravestone gives me hints, clues—even those that bear only a name. Most say more, though—*Beloved Husband and Father. Sister. Son. Wife. Friend.*

Some contain engravings that tell you a little about the person it honors: a cross, a flower, a barn, a dog, a book. And some these days even display actual pictures—I walk past one featuring a photo of a couple wearing Hawaiian leis, clearly on a cherished vacation. Down near a picturesque lake, I find the grave of a young man, the stone marker filled with the words of grieving parents clearly desperate for their son to be remembered as loving and kind. There are multiple images of him superimposed on the black marble. I wonder how he died.

That's always the missing part of the story—but I understand. We don't want people to be remembered for how they died but for how they lived.

As I wend my way around the connecting, curving lanes, eventually returning back to Aunt Nan's and Uncle Philip's, theirs is still the most decorated spot in the place. And there are stories in that, too, in every flower or decoration left on a grave. While I always thought extensively decorated graves said more about the person doing the decorating than the person buried there, I'm viewing that a little differently now, too. We're doing our best to honor them because they were worthy of remembrance and we don't want them to be forgotten. Now, in every filled vase I see love.

When Uncle Philip died, I was mournfully sad, and heartbroken for Aunt Nan. But now I'm heartbroken for me. And my mother. And Hannah. And anyone who knew what a bright light Aunt Nan shone into the world. Death has become an impossibly large mystery for me—I've spent more time in the last few months pondering what it all means and where a person's energy goes when it's no longer inside their body than ever in my life.

And decorating the graves is my solitary task now. Mom asked if I wanted her help since Aunt Nan can no longer be my companion in the endeavor. Ben offered, too. And maybe someday I'll take them up on it. But this was my thing with Aunt Nan, for just her and I alone. Now it's *still* my thing with Aunt Nan.

I plop down in the grass in front of the grave, remembering that strangely jarring phone call when Mom told me she was gone. It made no sense—none at all.

"That can't be," I told Mom. "I just saw her a few hours ago." I truly believed maybe she was mistaken and I wanted so desperately to make it true.

I could tell my words threw Mom. I guess it was hard enough news to deliver without someone arguing about it. Or maybe I made her believe it hadn't happened, too, if only for an instant. Still, she said, "It was sudden. An aneurysm."

"But—I mean..."

"She collapsed in Remke's." A local supermarket.

The strangest questions rolled through my mind. What was in her cart? Had she gotten a pot pie from the deli for dinner that night? She often picked up the market's pot pie or fried chicken if she didn't feel like cooking, and she timed her grocery shopping around the dinner hour so they'd still be hot when she got home.

I still wonder that now—what was in the cart? Did she have any clue she'd never eat dinner that night? Was she feeling happy, sad, tired, or anything else? She surely still wore the same lavender top I'd seen her in earlier that day when she hugged me so tight.

God, I'm so glad for that hug. For those 'I love you's.

A tear rolls down my cheek at the memories. Death is so strange. Over and over, I keep thinking: *She was just right here. As alive and vibrant as ever.*

And now—somehow—she's there. Under that grave marker and all the pumpkins and gourds I've placed at its base.

But I know she wouldn't want me to cry, so I try to wipe my tears and pull myself together and believe she's still with me somehow enjoying this beautiful fall day.

I read a book that said I should ask my departed loved one for a specific sign to let me know she's still with me in spirit, and though that might sound crazy, I spontaneously decide to do it right now.

Looking at the headstone, I say, "Aunt Nan, it seems like whenever something big is going on in my life, you've been there, either reassuring me I'm on the right path or leading me to answers I'm not sure I'd have found without you. So when I'm dealing with other big things in the future, can you send me a sign to let me know I'm on the right track?" The book said to make it something specific, something you'll know for sure is from your loved one, not just a cardinal or a dragonfly. So I spend a second thinking about what *she* loved and what *I* love, and I say, "Please send me...purple cats." She loved purple, I love cats. And I don't even know exactly what it is I'm asking for in a world where cats don't come in purple, but I figure I'll definitely know it when I see it.

If it even works. If she's even...anywhere.

If she is, she's probably laughing that I just asked for purple cats, whether or not the afterlife actually works in a way that allows her to deliver such a bizarre request.

And as I glance up the slight incline toward Grandpa Ed's grave, I find myself thinking back on that crazy day she sent me trudging up the hill to accost Ben with a fake question about a dog, and I laugh a little. It seems so long ago in so many ways. And in others, it feels like yesterday.

And I know, in my heart, what Ben and I need to do.

Ben

I'm sitting in one of the Adirondack chairs, looking out at the city. The Talcrita Tower has reach its full height in steel beams, and all that remains now is the finishing of it: the inside and the exterior. Each time I look at it, I know I'm leaving a mark. Which I guess is all most of us want to do, though the marks can be measured in countless ways.

But I can't say I feel happy inside, the way I used to. Daphne is running around the yard, chasing fallen leaves, Emma's curled up in the windowsill behind me, and my sweet wife will soon be home from the cemetery, where she goes even more since we lost Aunt Nan so unexpectedly.

Damn, I didn't see that coming. No one did.

And I worry for Haley. She used to bring the sunshine wherever she went—used to *be* the sunshine. Yet now I see her reeling from death. A plight I know well, but a plight I don't know how to coach her through because I never got very skilled at it myself.

Aunt Nan's passing has affected me, too. She wasn't in my life for that long, but I loved her. She brought me and Haley together. And she helped us in so many ways.

Sometimes I remember little moments with her. Like our wedding day when she so proudly gave us her mystery wedding gift. Or when she spilled her purse on the sidewalk to orchestrate my second meeting with Haley—I still can't believe I never figured out it was her until Haley told me.

I know Haley's life feels emptier without her, and mine does, too. I guess each person who falls away from us in death indeed leaves a void, just like Clarence the Angel explained to George in "It's a Wonderful Life." I feel Aunt Nan's void. And I wonder what might fill it.

Ruminating on the concept, I realize Haley filled a *huge* void in *my* life. I'd been in denial, but now I can see that maybe when we lose people, it balances things out if we add new ones. Haley said in her wedding vows that she and I balance each other—maybe we *all* give each other different degrees of balance.

As for the question of adoption, we tabled it when Aunt Nan died. There was suddenly a funeral to plan, family support to give, emotions to grapple with. And we've all been pitching in, going through Aunt Nan's belongings bit by bit, a taxing task. So it seemed wise to set aside the other big thing going on in our lives. Though I know it's still on Haley's mind. How could it *not* be?

My thoughts on the subject haven't changed, and I continue to feel like a jerk. It's easy right now, not talking about it, but it's still there, just under the surface. Until...I don't know when. I don't want to bring it up while Haley is dealing with loss. But at the same time, I don't like being the guy who just lets it ride, like I'm ignoring what's important to my wife just because we don't want the same thing.

If Aunt Nan were here, I'd probably ask her what to do at this point.

But if Aunt Nan were here, we wouldn't have tabled the discussion in the first place. And we'd have opened the wedding box.

When I hear the back door, I look up to see Haley. "Hey, babe," I say with a soft smile.

She returns it with a wave, making her way toward me. Daphne runs to greet her and she bends over to pet her, cooing, "Yes, hi, I missed you, too. Always such a ball of energy." Sliding into the chair next to me, she tosses me a playful grin. "The cat is so much easier."

Not used to seeing her in a good mood lately, it makes me laugh. "But the dog lets you know she loves you." We still do this sometimes—banter about the virtues of cats versus dogs, just to tease each other. "It's nice to see you smile," I add.

Rather than respond to that directly, she says pleasantly, "I want to open the box."

I sit up a little straighter, thrown. "Huh?" Talk about a curveball. "We're not even fighting about anything."

"That's the point," she says, holding up one triumphant finger. "Over and over, we almost open Aunt Nan's gift, but something *always* stops us. I'm starting to think we're *never* going to open it based on a disagreement."

"That might be true," I agree.

"And it would be a nice way to honor her. We can finally see what she wanted to give us. That simple."

I can't deny it makes sense. And it sounds...healing. "Okay," I say, nodding. "Let's see what Aunt Nan gave us, once and for all."

"One last gift from her."

22

Opening the Wedding Box

Haley

It feels almost surreal to tear the cream-colored paper away. We sit at the kitchen table, me on one side, Ben on the other. Daphne and Emma both sit strangely at attention nearby, watching the ceremonial unwrapping almost as if they can sense the gravity of the moment. It's the first time I've started opening this box that I've felt calm, sure, at peace. It's almost as if Aunt Nan is in the room with us.

I tear the paper slowly, so that you can hear each long rip, my eyes occasionally meeting Ben's. The rest of the time, we're staring at the box being revealed before us. I can hear my own heartbeat.

When the paper falls away and my fingers curve around the lid on both sides, I ask, "Ready?"

He just nods.

And this feels...sacred. Like we're taking the lid off the Holy Grail. Aunt Nan's Holy Grail.

Inside: Envelopes. Strewn about.

I guess I'm not surprised—the box was never heavy—but it's not the grand unveiling we both anticipated.

"Hmm..." Ben murmurs.

"How do we...?" I begin uncertainly, looking at them all—mostly common plain white envelopes, of different shapes, a few colored ones mixed in.

"Just dig in, I guess," Ben says.

And so we do. "I'll go first." I pluck out a white envelope on top and, taking a deep breath, run my index finger along the flap, opening it. My heart officially feels as if it's going to leap from my chest.

Reaching inside, I pull out...a $20 gift card for a popular pizza chain.

I hold it up—and we both laugh. We laugh uproariously. I lean back in my chair, laughing harder than I have in months. "Oh my gosh," I squeal through my laughter.

"Gift cards!" Ben says. "All this time, waiting to open the box, and it's a bunch of gift cards!"

"Well," I say, still amused, "I guess we'll be eating free for a while."

That's when I see something else in the same envelope and pull it out. I unfold a small slip of paper to find a handwritten note: *Treat yourselves to a pizza! With every slice, share something you love about each other.*

I show Ben and we smile at each other. "I guess not *just* gift cards," he says. And I know we're both thinking the same thing: Sweet Aunt Nan. Nothing about a bunch of gift cards is going to fix anyone's marital problems, but a pizza that comes with an appreciation exercise surely can't hurt.

It would be easy to be disappointed after so much buildup—buildup we created ourselves, I might add—and yet, what were we expecting? Some miraculous, glowing solution to the world's problem like when Indiana Jones opened the Ark of the Covenant? This gift is classic Aunt Nan in every way, so we'll gladly enjoy it for what it is.

We take turns opening envelopes.

We find a gift card for a couples' massage with a note that says: *Let all your tensions go and use the time to remember how much you love each other.*

We get one for our favorite chili parlor: *Let a hot and spicy meal rekindle your affection.*

We discover another for DeGregorio's: *A visit to your favorite restaurant will bring back good memories and create new ones at the same time!*

We open gift cards for the movie theatre: *Good for one rom-com or feel-good flick! Whatever is wrong between you, let it go and laugh a while instead!*

And on it goes—gift cards for everything from fast food to a shoe store. (*Let a new a pair of tennis shoes remind you that you chose to walk side-by-side through life.*)

"Well, these are gonna keep us busy for a while," Ben says with a smile.

"And it'll be lots of fun." I'm smiling, too, feeling Aunt Nan's generous love all around us.

"It's actually a great gift," he concedes. And I can't argue the point. Had we not waited so long or made such a big deal of it, we'd have found this an *amazing* gift—creative, thoughtful, and practical all at the same time.

Then Ben pulls something else from the box, a bunch of

small sheets of paper stapled together. On the top one, red hearts surround words written in red Magic Marker: *Love Coupons.* We both laugh.

"Wow—she made us coupon books," he says, and pulls out a second one, decorated in pink. "One for each of us."

Inside, old-fashioned handmade coupons we can present to each other: *This coupon good for one back rub. This coupon good for one kiss. This coupon entitles the bearer to pick the movie.* And so on. As Ben thumbs through his, he stops at one near the back and laughs.

"What?" I ask.

He holds it out to show me. *Good for one jelly donut.* "I guess you told her about our jelly donut thing."

I think back, pursing my lips. "I'm not sure I did. I mean, I don't remember ever mentioning it to *anyone.*"

Something about that makes me decide to look more closely through my own book. The last one says: *Good for one bouquet of daisies.* I hold it up to show him.

"Well," he says, "they're your favorite flower. She probably knew that."

Again, though, I find myself trying to think back through every conversation with Aunt Nan about every tiny little thing. "Maybe," I say. "Although, really, it's not something I talk about, not something people know about me." I shrug. "Though I guess it's not unreasonable to think she knew. The jelly donut thing, though, is...more surprising."

He nods, looking puzzled. "How on earth could she have known?"

"How on earth did she know there was a house for sale

on Blissful Lane? How on earth did she know *everything* she knew?"

Since there is, of course, no answer to that question, Ben just lets out a small, perplexed sigh, then turns his attention back to the box. "Okay, one more envelope at the bottom and it's a biggie."

I watch as he pulls out a six-by-nine-inch manila envelope. Together, we read the rather lengthy note written on it:

Inside is a letter for each of you. You are to read them privately and not share the contents of your letter with each other—ever. These are my private, personal thoughts and advice written expressly to you, Haley, and to you, Ben, to help you get through the ups and downs of marriage.

"Well, that kinda sucks," Ben says.

I flinch in surprise. "What do you mean? I think it's coolly mysterious."

He raises his eyebrows. "Honestly, I've had enough mystery for a lifetime where this box is concerned. I wasn't expecting more secrets. Especially between you and me."

I just shrug, though. "Don't think of it as a secret. It's just as if we we're each having a private conversation with her. Stuff she thought will resonate specifically with you and stuff she felt will resonate more with me. And we really *do* have to *never* tell each other what they say."

He gives his head a skeptical tilt. "Even if it's nothing important?"

"No matter *what* it says," I insist. "Because it was important to *her*."

He nods, seeing my point. "Okay, agreed."

Unsealing the manila envelope, Ben pulls out two smaller

envelopes, one pale green, with his name written on the outside, and a pink one addressed to me. He hands mine over, then asks, "Read them right here, right now? Or later, by ourselves?"

"Right here, right now," I say. "Just no peeking."

Another nod from my husband and we both open our envelopes.

Then my world narrows to what I find inside mine: old-fashioned sheets of lined stationery with a row of delicate flowers across the top, the rest of the space filled with Aunt Nan's familiar handwriting. Somehow the very sight of her script draws me in, making me feel as if she *is* still with us, as if she could have written it just yesterday.

Her handwriting has been on everything else in the box, too, but like so many things since her death, having a whole letter from her, such a big piece of her heart in my very hands, makes me feel the tremendous loss and a beautiful connection to her at the very same time, along with that emotion I've experienced over and over: *She was just right here.*

I take a deep breath and begin to read.

My dearest Haley,

I'm so happy you found the love of your life in Ben—he's exactly the special sort of man you deserve. I know in my heart that your love will be everlasting.

But if you're reading this, it means you've discovered that marriage sometimes becomes a bumpy road. Two hearts, no matter how closely entwined, will occasionally end up in a snarled knot that needs untangling. Perhaps that's the risk of letting ourselves become entwined in love—some tangles are an inevitable result, but they come with too many rewards not to take the risk.

So I ask you now to take whatever in your marriage you may be angry or sad or frustrated about, and just put that away for a few minutes. Instead fill your heart with thoughts of the many wondrous things you love about Ben. Celebrate your love for him in your mind.

Have you done that? Good. Now, come back to your current disagreement. Whatever it is made you open the box, and this letter. You probably feel strongly about whatever is.

But now I give you another task. Put yourself in Ben's shoes. Stop and ask yourself: Why does he feel differently than I do? What inside him is causing that? Can you see his side? Can you feel what's in his heart?

And now, my dear niece, I ask for one more thing: This once, if there's any way you can feel what's in Ben's heart enough to just honor it, to let go of your own wants, to be the bigger person, the one who gives of her own heart to connect with her partner, do it.

I know what I'm suggesting isn't easy—and maybe you'll find you can't, but if you can, it'll be the purest act of love you can give your husband. It will show him how much you love him, how much you believe in your marriage. Even if you have to give something up, it'll clear the way for love and joy and miracles to rush in and surround you both. I promise.

All my love,
Aunt Nan

Ben

My dearest Ben,

I'm so happy you found the love of your life in Haley—she's exactly the special sort of woman you deserve. I know in my heart that your love will be everlasting.

But if you're reading this, it means you've discovered that marriage sometimes becomes a bumpy road. Two hearts, no matter how closely entwined, will occasionally end up in a snarled knot that needs untangling. Perhaps that's the risk of letting ourselves become entwined in love—some tangles are an inevitable result, but they come with too many rewards not to take the risk.

So I ask you now to take whatever in your marriage you may be angry or sad or frustrated about, and just put that away for a few minutes. Instead fill your heart with thoughts of the many wondrous things you love about Haley. Celebrate your love for her in your mind.

Have you done that? Good. Now, come back to your current disagreement. Whatever it is made you open the box, and this letter. You probably feel strongly about whatever is.

But now I give you another task. Put yourself in Haley's shoes. Stop and ask yourself: Why does she feel differently than I do? What inside her is causing that? Can you see her side? Can you feel what's in her heart?

And now, my dear nephew, I ask for one more thing: This once, if there's any way you can feel what's in Haley's heart enough to just honor it, to let go of your own wants, to be the bigger person, the one who gives of his own heart to connect with his partner, do it.

I know what I'm suggesting isn't easy—and maybe you'll find you can't, but if you can, it'll be the purest act of love you can give your wife. It will show her how much you love her, how much you believe in your marriage. Even if you have to give something up, it'll clear the way for love and joy and miracles to rush in and surround you both. I promise.

All my love,
Aunt Nan

I sit and stare at the letter—in fact, I read it over several times. Haley sits right across the table with her own letter, and while I thought I'd burn with curiosity to know what hers says, instead I'm completely caught up in Aunt Nan's message to *me*.

It's true that I get so wrapped up in what *I* want that maybe I don't truly consider *why* Haley wants something or how it might affect her happiness not to have it. Maybe all of us do that. Maybe it gets hard to see the marital forest for all of our personal trees.

And when I do what Aunt Nan asks of me—stopping, seeing the world through my wife's sweet, loving eyes—I do begin to feel what she wants and why.

I feel it deep in my gut.

In a way that makes me know I can't keep it from her.

It hits me like a ton of bricks that I've been selfish and thoughtless and uncaring—too caught up in my own issues to remember to take care of my wife's heart.

I look up from the letter still clutched in my fist to meet her gaze across the table. I see the girl I fell in love with, I see the woman she's grown into. I see her impulsiveness, her humor, her sensitivities, her kindness, her whole heart.

We both speak at the same time. Just as I blurt out, "We can adopt a baby," she says, "We don't have to have kids to be happy."

23

Haley and Ben's Five-Year Anniversary

Haley

I've never been cautious with my heart. In a world where a heart can be broken in so many ways, perhaps that seems downright reckless, and yet my heart remains, I suppose, an eternal optimist.

Once upon a time I tortured my heart by believing in the good intentions of every boy I met. Now, I torture my heart by having become a hoarder of pregnancy tests. Despite what the doctor said. Despite knowing the odds. Because every time my period is a little late, I have to wonder, and it makes me eager to take a test. So I tend to just pick up one or two when I notice them on the drugstore shelf. Just in case. I have a collection of probably ten or twelve going right now.

You'd think I'd just accept that my body is changing and I'm not as regular as I used to be. You'd think I'd quit torturing myself since, if I got pregnant, I would eventually figure it out if I just waited for more clues, like, say, being more than two days overdue, which is usually about the time I whip out a little white stick and pee on it.

But I guess it's just that minute of excited hope and anticipation, the lingering belief that maybe, just maybe, somehow, it'll happen. Sure, that excitement gets tied up in gloom and despair even as I'm taking the test, but...well, that's where I am.

Today is our fifth wedding anniversary. And my period, technically, was due yesterday. It seems like a good enough reason to check. Especially since my parents are having a celebration for us tonight at their place. As I open the box and do the deed, I fantasize about making a grand announcement tonight. *Guess what, everyone? We're pregnant! Even though the doctor said we couldn't be! It's an anniversary miracle!*

Although, seriously, if I'm pregnant, can I possibly hold it in until the party? That's three whole hours away! If that stick turns blue, I'll be on the phone to all pertinent parties, and possibly the local news. But wow—what a celebration that would make for tonight! And Ben would be so, so happy! I sigh joyfully, imagining.

And then I look at the stick. Negative.

I blow out a dejected breath, mad at myself for the fantasy. I guess this level of desperation—pregnancy test after unwarranted pregnancy test, just shows how bad I want it.

Ben has no idea I do this. I'm not hiding it—the whole collection of pregnancy tests openly resides under my side of the bathroom sink. But I guess guys aren't very observant about women's bathroom products. And I see no reason to draw him into my unrealistically wishful delusion. One deluded person in a relationship is more than enough.

Just as I drop the stick in the wastebasket, my phone rings. It's Sienna. "Hey," I answer as I make my way into the greatroom.

"Happy anniversary!" she shouts ever-so-merrily as I plop down onto the couch with the cat.

"Thanks," I say, reaching out to stroke Emma's fur for comfort. "Are you coming tonight?"

"Of course—I just had some time and figured we haven't chatted in a while. But why do you sound sad?"

Darn perceptive best friend. I haven't told Sienna—or anyone—about the tests, either. Maybe I should—but won't it make me sound like a lunatic unwilling to accept the truth? So I'm just *partly* honest. "Okay—you caught me feeling down about not being able to get pregnant."

She stays quiet for a moment, until she finally says, "I haven't want to pry, but...I thought Ben gave you the green light to adopt last fall after you opened Aunt Nan's gift."

I take a deep breath, tired before even trying to explain. "He did. But when we both gave in to each other, it created a huge conundrum. I can't honor *his* offer without it taking away *my* offer, and vice versa."

"Oh, wow," Sienna says. "Very 'Gift of the Magi.' Sort of."

"So as truly beautiful and heartening as the moment was," I go on, "ultimately, it just left us in the same predicament where we started—only in a much more loving way. Which is nice, don't get me wrong. But it didn't actually lead anywhere. I suspect Aunt Nan didn't bargain on *both* of us being so reasonable. Or...she knew we would, but just figured it would make us be nice to each other and then things would work themselves out."

"How did you leave things after that?"

I sigh at the irony of what I'm about to say. "We actually argued over it a few times—the opposite way as we started. Ben insisting we look into adoption and me insisting we shouldn't." I sink a little more deeply into the couch—seriously, this has been mentally exhausting. "Finally, we agreed to just let it float for a while and see if it somehow leads to an answer."

"I'm afraid that's not good odds for you," she points out. "You can let it float forever and have no adoption. If I were you, I'd let go of the Gift of the Magi aspect of it and accept his offer. If he made it honestly, he won't mind."

"Hannah said the same thing," I tell her. Then I stop, search my heart. I search it a lot these days, yet I always end up in the same place. "But I can't. My offer was made honestly, too, and if I accept his, it makes mine feel less valid."

"Well, all I can say is, you're a good wife. Most women in your position would snap up that offer in a heartbeat. And I'm sorry you're sad on your anniversary."

"Well, I'm gonna snap out of it—right now," I declare. "We're having a party tonight, after all. And just like at the holidays, Aunt Nan won't be there and we'll all miss her and be trying to compensate, so I need to put on my best, happiest face. And I have to remember—I have an amazing life. And if I'm not meant to be a mother...well, Aunt Nan took a lot of joy in being an aunt—so can I."

The wisteria is in full bloom on the arbor in my parents' backyard, reminiscent of our wedding day. Mom has decorated the patio beautifully even though it's only a small gathering of our closest friends and family. I can't help but be cheered up.

We host most summer gatherings at *our* house now—the view never gets old—but being back at my girlhood home reminds me how far I've come in life. Revisiting the spot where we got married, five years later, really makes me feel how far Ben and I have come as a couple, as well. The baby issue notwithstanding, we've built a wonderful home, the bakery is thriving and Ben's career is going gangbusters, we have our fur babies to come home to each night—and we still love each other like crazy.

From the arbor, I look over to see all the people we care most about. Dad and Dan man the grill, Dad in a silly *Kiss the Cook* apron I gave him when I was twelve. Mom, Hannah, and Olivia are arranging other food on a long table. Terrence plays with Cole and his own little one, Wyatt, near the lake, while Sienna, predictably, snaps pictures. Cora, one step away from adolescence now, is tapping on the back window at Puff on the other side.

"What's up, Mrs. Page?" Ben's arms close around me from behind and his breath warms my ear.

I cover his hands with mine and tell him, "I was thinking I'm a lucky woman."

"Funny, I was just thinking I'm a lucky man," he says on a soft laugh.

"No regrets?" I ask. "About marrying me? There was a time you were weird about commitment, you know."

"But I got over it fast, if you recall. I knew you were the right girl all along—I was just...in a little immature denial."

I nod and get more serious. "I shouldn't have said you were weird about commitment. You had your reasons."

He peers down at me lovingly. "Reasons or not, I'd be a far less happy man without you. You know that, right?"

I nod. Because I do. And when he leans down to kiss me, it reminds me of the magic between us. Just like Aunt Nan's letter reminded me of it. We're so much more than the things that can threaten to come between us.

"Oh my God, you'd think these two were newlyweds," Terrence teases loudly, drawing attention to us.

I blush and everyone chuckles.

Dad announces dinner is ready, adding, "Come and get it while it's hot!" So we all make our way to the table, beautifully set in our lilac-and-white wedding colors. As we sit down, Ben thanks Mom and Dad for the celebration, and I take a little fresh joy at having given him a family.

Dad lifts a glass and says, "To Ben and Haley and the first five years of their forever!"

Everyone toasts, glasses clink, and people say, "Hear, hear."

After sips are taken, Dad's glass is back in the air. "And to Nan, who isn't here with us today." She's been gone a year now.

We all go quiet until Hannah says, "But she'd be happy we're having a party, and she's with us in spirit."

As we begin to eat, I think maybe this one-year mark is

when I'll finally get used to her absence, finally accept it. But on the other hand, maybe I *never* want to stop feeling her or missing her.

As we enjoy a delicious meal—ribs and chicken, along with baked potatoes and corn on the cob—I'm undeniably aware that we're the only couple here without children. And I suffer pangs of envy—even as I watch Olivia struggle to get toddler Wyatt to eat, not getting to eat much herself because of it. But at the same time, if this is our life, I can handle it. I'll just have to apologize to everyone in advance if I become that person who forces her pets to wear Santa hats in holiday photos in lieu of having children to dress in matching outfits.

Mom is on her feet, going around refilling wineglasses. "Were you red or white, Hannah?" she asks my sister.

"Oh, none for me tonight," Hannah says.

Like Mom, I hadn't noticed Hannah was drinking only water until right now. "Why not and since when?" I ask. It's no secret that my sister loves wine.

She shrugs. "Just cutting back."

It doesn't ring true.

And that's when Dan says, under his breath, "Honey, just tell them."

"No," she whispers adamantly.

Dan rolls his eyes like she's being silly and says, "What's the big deal?"

Hannah still speaks low. "This is Haley and Ben's night."

"Just tell us what?" Dad asks, tuning in to the conversation late.

No one answers, though all eyes are on my sister and her husband now. She looks disgruntled and he appears sheepish.

"Well?" Mom says. "What's the big secret?"

Finally, Dan says, "We got some news today. We're having another baby."

I sink into the bricks of the patio.

Everyone else at the table is saying all the appropriate things, and it's clear my parents are—understandably—excited. Another grandchild. Yay. But I, on the other hand, can't muster a word because I feel like a flower closing up. I'm happy for my sister, I really am. I'm just a little broken right now.

Next to me, Ben is among those handing out congratulations, but his are more awkward, pained. This is killing us both and we feel like jerks about it. I'm looking down, into the pastel napkin in my lap, and my eyes ache as I try not to cry. Crying at your sister's good news is the worst.

That's when my mother asks, "Haley, honey, are you okay?"

Crap. I can't even look up. Finally, I push back my chair and say, "Excuse me."

That's when Dan, at last, catches on. Everyone here knows we can't have kids. "Oh God, I'm sorry—I didn't even think."

"It's okay," I mutter like a teenager running from some adolescent embarrassment as I make a beeline for the house.

Ben follows me. And I love him for it. Because we might disagree on some things, but the one thing we know about each other is how much we wish we could make a baby together.

"Babe, it's okay," he says once we're inside, away from people.

And I'm safe to finally let the tears fall. I'm wiping them away, sniffling, barreling through the house with no real destination until I reach the front foyer, where I reach for tissues on a table, grateful it's only my husband and me right now. "I know," I blubber. "I just..."

"Babe," he says to me, "we can adopt. Really."

Oh, my sweet Ben, feeling my pain and hating to see me suffer. But I need to be stronger. Three minutes ago, I was okay with not having kids. Hannah's news just threw me when I least expected it. So I shake my head. "That's sweet of you, honey, but it's not what you really want."

"I want what *you* want."

It's a truly loving sentiment—but honestly, the whole situation has come to seem impossible. Complicated emotionally and every other way, too. So I shake my head again. "What if you're right that the process is nightmarish, and what if we put our whole hearts into it and it still never comes to be?" After all this time, I've suddenly developed the instinct to guard my heart. I crush my eyes shut in despair. "Ben, I just don't know what to do."

Ben

I take Haley in my arms, wanting desperately to comfort her. It was such a nice party until this news. And of course we're happy for Hannah and Dan. We love their kids and will love this new one, too. It just stings, under the circumstances.

Haley is my family now, the cornerstone of my life. Even if the last couple of years have held some challenges: losing Aunt Nan, and the frustration about the baby, or lack thereof.

I meant it when I said we could adopt. I mean it *every* time I say it. But when I try to give her what she wants more than anything, she shoots me down. I just don't know how to make her happy here. And right now, all I can do I hold her.

When the doorbell rings, we both flinch—and then separate, like kids caught making out on a dark dance floor. "Who could that be?" she mutters.

I don't answer it yet, waiting as she dries her eyes and presses down the skirt of her sundress, pulling herself together for the unexpected visitor.

When I open the door, Pastor Tom is standing on the other side.

"Haley, Ben!" he greets us, clearly happy to see us.

"Hi, Tom," I say.

Despite her efforts, he immediately zeroes in on the fact that Haley isn't her usual, cheerful self. "Have I come at a bad time?" he asks, appearing concerned.

"No," she insists, sniffing back a last tear. "It's fine."

"Are you sure? Because I can go." He points over his shoulder. Along with the rest of the family, we've now made Pastor Tom feel awkward, as well.

But Haley insists. "No, really. I'm good. It's nice to see you. Please come in."

As Pastor Tom steps into the foyer, he still looks uncertain as he says, "I came over when I saw your car in the driveway. It's fortuitous you're here because I was just about to call you."

Well, this is a surprise. Tom officiated our wedding, and the whole family is friendly with him since he lives next door, but we haven't talked to him since the wedding day other than the occasional brief exchange about his dog or the weather. Haley's expression tells me she's as perplexed as I am.

"Can we sit down?" Tom asks.

"Sure," I say, anxiously ushering the three of us into the living room. We've had enough surprises tonight already. So as soon as we're all seated, I ask, "What's up?"

But he hesitates—in a way that suggests it's a delicate issue. *Just spit it out, Tom,* I want to snap—but I hold my tongue.

Finally, he begins, "Haley, your mother has shared with me the fact that you and Ben haven't been able to conceive."

Wow. Really? More on *this* tonight?

Haley just nods. And I'm thinking that if he's here to counsel us or something, I might need to shut it down. I'm not anti-therapy, but this might not be the time.

Instead, though, he shocks the hell out of us by saying, "There's a baby."

"What?" Haley murmurs, her confusion echoing my own.

"I know of a baby," he says, "who needs a good home."

Neither of us replies. I think we're both numb. Or fearful. Or any number of other things.

Tom goes on, though. "The baby is six weeks old and his parents were killed in an auto accident last week. The baby's mother was from Korea, with no family. The father was American, and his parents are parishioners of mine. They initially thought they'd keep and raise the baby boy, but she's in a wheelchair, and they've decided it's just too much for them, understandably.

"They came to me for counsel, advice. They're interested in a private adoption, and would feel much better about their decision if they're in control of the process—if they can meet the adoptive parents and feel sure the baby is going to a good home. I thought immediately of you two.

"There would be a home study, of course, which is an expense, and there would be legal fees, but after the home study is concluded, the baby would be yours. His name, by the way, is Jackson."

Then Tom looks directly at me. "Ben, I understand from Nina that you've had reservations about adopting, so if this is an unwanted offer or out-of-line in any way, I apologize. But as I say, when I met this sweet baby boy, I couldn't help thinking of you. And—"

"We'll take him," I cut him off to say. "Of course, we'll take him."

Because my world changed the second I heard the words "killed in an auto accident." This baby, this boy...is me. Not exactly, certainly. But...what else would I do? What else *could* I do? Who would ever understand this child like I will? Who else will know what's missing in his life, or the questions he'll ask, the things he'll wonder about. And while there are probably a million people who would be happy to adopt him, I'm probably the very best parent he could have, knowing what I know, being where I've been. I can't risk for a second that he ever feel alone in the world, or like something's missing, or that he not experience the joy of a big, loving family.

Haley says to me, "Are you sure, Ben? Truly?"

I feel myself nodding repeatedly. "Absolutely. One-hundred percent."

Tom breathes a sigh of relief, and for the first time since his arrival, he smiles. "Jackson's grandparents were excited for me to reach out when I told them what a great couple you are. They're eager to get the ball rolling. If you're both certain, we could go meet them—and Jackson—right now."

24

Haley

Ben and I burst through the backdoor onto my parents' patio. Before I can get a word out, though, they're all looking at me like I'm a fragile flower—okay, fair, because sometimes I am—and Dan is on his feet, coming toward me. "Haley, I'm so sorry. I'm such an idiot."

"It's okay," I tell him. "But we have to go now."

"No, it's not," he insists.

And Mom is saying, "Oh, please don't leave. This is your party, your anniversary!"

Both of them are making a move to hug me, which is sweet and all, but I just don't have time for that right now. "It really is okay, I promise," I say to Dan.

"She means it," Ben says behind me. "Everything is great, actually." I can almost hear the excitement bubbling in his voice. And I'm again struck with shock that he *wants this!*

"Then why are you leaving?" Dad asks, also on his feet now.

"I'm sorry, too," Hannah chimes in, and it's clear the whole lot of them are up in arms over our hasty departure.

"You have nothing to be sorry for," I tell her, "but I need you all to be quiet and listen for a minute. A miraculous thing just happened."

Collectively, they go all wide-eyed and slack-jawed. "What?" My mom asks.

"Tom came to the front door," Ben tells them.

"What for?" Dad asks.

"He has a baby for us," I tell them. The words come out sounding strange to me, soft, surreal. Saying it out loud throws me into a deeper state of shock.

"What?"

"A baby?"

"What do you mean?"

Ben takes over. "Someone at his church has a baby who lost his parents' suddenly and he needs a home."

"And that's you guys," Hannah says, her eyes warm and bright and filled with joy.

I nod, and I finally let myself smile. "I can't believe it." I shake my head. "I mean, it just came out of nowhere."

"That's amazing!" My mother says, clasping her hands together. Then she comes to hug me again and this time I let her.

"Thing is," Ben goes on, "we're going meet the baby and his grandparents—like right now. That's why we have to go."

"Oh my goodness," Mom says.

"Wow," I hear Terrence murmur, clearly as stunned as

everyone else. Maybe *more* stunned that Ben is so on board, knowing him so well. And that makes two of us, but I'm not arguing about it. I guess my heart understands why—the way the baby lost his parents. But my head is too full of astonishment and anticipation and a million other things to think through it very carefully right now.

"Well, go!" Hannah says, shooing us away. "But call me later."

"Me, too!" Mom says.

"Me three," comes from Sienna.

Terrence adds, "Dude, check in with me after, okay?"

And then we're back inside and I'm grabbing up my purse and we're rushing out the front door where Tom is waiting to drive us.

I slide into the front seat next to him and Ben hops in back. Emotion roils inside me and I feel like a volcano about to overflow.

"Ready?" Tom says with a pastorly smile.

"Absolutely," Ben says.

Though as Tom starts driving up the street, I turn to him and erupt. "Tom, I gotta be honest—I'm starting to freak out here."

"That's understandable, Haley—you just got a huge and unexpected piece of news. Take some deep breaths."

Easy for him to say. My heart is beating like a drum against my chest—I'm dumbfounded that this is happening and beginning to feel overwhelmed by it. I mean, ten minutes ago we were childless and mentally preparing to stay that way for a lifetime. Now we're in a car going to meet our baby? *Our* baby? Our. Baby.

"What if they don't like us?" I spew. "What if we're not what they're expecting or hoping for? I wouldn't have worn such a low-cut dress if I'd known I was getting interviewed as an adoptive parent tonight."

Next to me, Tom laughs good-naturedly as if we're just on some kind of pleasant joyride here and I've made a cute joke. Neither could be further from the truth. "It's all right, Haley. You look lovely—summery and pretty. And they know you've had no warning. I reminded them of that when I called while you were out back. They understand how surprised you are."

Over the seat, Ben is squeezing my shoulder, saying, "It's all right, babe. It really is. They'll love you. They'll love me, too. How could they not?"

Even so, I say to Tom, "I feel so unprepared. For making someone *like* me. For suddenly having a baby with no warning. We don't have any baby supplies. I don't know how to be a mom."

But good old Pastor Tom—he can't be ruffled. He just keeps smiling and reassuring me, "You have nothing to worry about, I promise. Ken and Jean are both kind people who will see the same in you immediately. And remember, the home study has to be completed before the adoption takes place. You'll have some time to get things in order."

I nod, trying to shake off my anxiety. It doesn't work, though. Because as thrilled as I am by this turn of events, I'm stung with a hundred unanticipated fears. What if I meet this baby and don't feel a connection to him? It's not like we can just go to the baby store and pick out the one that speaks to us the most. I guess that's true for everyone—no one gets to *select* their baby—but for the first time I'm wondering if, in the world of adoption, anyone ever meets their baby and just doesn't feel they...hit it off, for lack of a better phrase. And what if Ken and Jean don't like something about us? What if *they* don't feel a connection—with *us*? And what if this baby somehow...doesn't like us? What if he instinctively knows we're fakes—not his real mom and dad—and rejects us in some way?

All relatively stupid questions, but that's where my head is as we drive.

Less than ten minutes later, we enter a community of small, mid-century cottages. It's a quiet neighborhood, but the houses are pressed close together and some are in want of care.

Soon Tom pulls into the cracked driveway of a little house with faded yellow siding, a sagging metal awning, and a wheelchair ramp where front steps used to be.

As the three of us make our way onto the front porch, I feel fifty shades of awkward. Like I'm out baby shopping in my low-cut strappy dress. Why didn't I bring a sweater? Ben must sense it because he reaches out to take my hand, giving a reassuring squeeze. "Be happy," he whispers to me. "This is meant to be."

I wish I felt as sure. I hate that I'm harboring doubts. I wish I'd had time to wrap my head around this, to even think about what to say to these people.

A moment later, a slight, gray-haired man is holding an old screen door open to let us inside. The living room is dark —dark wallpaper, dark carpet, dark furniture too big for the space. "Ken, Jean"—Tom motions to an older lady in a reclining chair—"this is Ben and Haley, who I've told you about."

Jean's smile is sweet and warm, like that of a loving grandma, as she holds her hand out to me. I follow the impulse to step forward and take it in mine. "It's so nice to meet you. You're as pretty as Tom said."

"That's very sweet of you," I tell her. "And we're so very sorry about your son and his wife."

Jean just nods, no words. I get it—her grief is fresh, and even though her son was an adult, I think of all the parents of all the children in the cemetery and know she's dealing with something unthinkable. It makes me squeeze her hand, cover it with my other one. I like her instantly and wish I could fix the things wrong in her life.

We exchange only a few more pleasantries before the soft cry of an infant cuts through our conversation and I realize the baby has been in the room with us the whole time. A small crib sits in a corner, but I saw only blankets inside it, not the baby covered by them. As we all look in that direction, Ken says, "Jackson must be waking up from his nap."

If my thumping heart had started to calm down while talking to Ken and Jean, now it's back at it, amplified in my ears. Everything I'm feeling must show on my face because Jean says to me, "Go ahead. Go on over and say hello."

Ben and I exchange looks, and he places his hand at the small of my back, guiding me over. We make our way, gingerly, taking a few steps that feel like a mile.

"Turn that on so you can see," Ken instructs, motioning to a floor lamp next to the crib.

Ben reaches over, clicks a switch, and the crib below is lit.

Inside, a sweet-looking baby stares silently up at me. He has black hair, dark eyes, and a certain gentleness emanating from him as I soak in that soft, powdery baby smell. And then my heart swells, like the Grinch's when it grew three sizes and busted through that little box around it—it's expanding in my chest, almost overwhelming my senses.

I blow out a breath I hadn't realized I was holding. Maybe I've been holding it, in some way or another, for a very long time, because it's suddenly as if I can breathe again, suddenly as if life makes sense again, suddenly as if there's purpose and hope and love all around me.

I reach my index finger down toward the baby's little hand, a move made as part of a wish, I suppose, but I'm still gobsmacked when he wraps his tiny little fingers around my much bigger one. I gasp and Ben lets out a soft sigh.

That's when I realize that the little yellow blanket wrapped around the baby has purple cat faces on it. I cover my mouth with my free hand, trying to hold in my reaction. But my heart is back to pounding in my ears now—only this time in a good way. A perfect way.

I whisper gently to my husband, "This is our baby."

It's a crisp, sunny October day when the adoption is complete and Ben and I bring Jackson Edward Page home with us. We kept Jackson's first name, because we like it and it already feels like part of him, but we changed his middle name to honor Ben's grandpa. Ken and Jean like that we were honoring someone we've lost. We're having a welcome party for friends and family next week, but for tonight, it's just us.

The last few months have been a whirlwind—getting the house ready, passing the home study, and counting down the days until Jackson became our son. And now that the day is here, my heart is soaring. I'm still not sure how to be a mommy, but I have Hannah and Mom to give me pointers, and I've visited with Jackson at Ken and Jean's house as often as possible without feeling pushy, so I've had plenty of holding and feeding and playtime with him already.

Now we're in the backyard, relaxing after a big day with glasses of lemonade, and introducing Jackson to his furry dog sister. I'm grateful to have such gentle pets as I watch Daphne raising her head to sniff sweetly at the newcomer in the handheld carrier. She's an eager, playful dog most of the time, but she seems to sense when it's time to be more gentle and circumspect. Inside, Emma, too, studied and sniffed, and seemed to understand that this is a new addition to our family—even if Ben clearly thought I was crazy when I said that.

Ben can't stop looking at the baby, and neither can I. Funny, it's usually the city skyline that holds his focus, but I guess we've finally found something that can vie for his attention.

Or...maybe he'll just combine them, since, as I take a sip of lemonade, I watch as Ben picks up the baby and points his little face toward the cityscape. "See that building?" he says to Jackson. "The dark, glass, curvy one?" The Talcrita Tower was finally completed and opened to corporate tenants a few months ago. "Daddy designed that. And you're never gonna stop hearing about it your whole life."

I laugh, and in that moment fall in love with him all over again—but this time I fall in love with him as a daddy. And I'm already in love with Jackson, too. Sure, a part of me knows challenges lie ahead: diapers to change, illnesses to get through, and a million other hurtles. But I'm so filled with happiness right now that I know everything will be okay. I guess I've started learning how to be a mom. And while in one way I'm sad Aunt Nan isn't here to meet our new son, in another I know she is. I have a purple-cat-face-covered blankie to prove it.

"I'll be right back," I say to Ben. "I drank too much lemonade too fast."

I'm so happy that I nearly dance my way into the house—singing under my breath randomly to the tune of *La Cucaracha*, "We have a baby, and I'm a mommy. We have a sweet little baby boy!"

As I pass a calendar hanging on our kitchen wall, my eyes fall on today's date, which has written on it in big red Magic Marker: *Baby Day!*, and it hits me that I'm a day or two late on my period. Truth is, I'm late every month now. But I still take the pregnancy tests out of sheer habit, since ya never know.

So I merrily murmur, "What the heck," and grab a test before I use the restroom. The whole pregnancy issue barely matters anymore, but I may as well use them up.

A minute later, the stick turns blue.

That can't be, of course. The stick never turns blue.

Because I can't get pregnant. Right?

I even blink a few times to make sure I really see what I

think I'm seeing. I just stare at it, trying to wrap my head around the situation.

Then I wonder if I can possibly muster up some more pee to take another test, which I'm certain will put this silliness to rest. I've never tested positive before, but I'm sure over-the-counter tests can't be a hundred percent accurate all the time.

So I guzzle some water, a whole bottle. Then I get another test from under the sink and use it.

A minute later, this one turns blue, too. And my heart starts beating fast again. I'm not even sure what I feel, it's such a shock.

Kind of like the *last time* I found out I was getting a baby.

I'm not sure what to do with this new information. Because...two tests. Two tests can't be wrong, right? And that's when the reality really hits me and I murmur, "Whoa."

Then I take my two tests and walk back outside to where Ben and Jackson are still bonding over the view. And I say, "Um, Ben?"

He turns to me with a smile. "Yeah?"

I hold out the tests. "I think I'm pregnant."

His eyes go wide, looking at the sticks, and then they raise to my face. We're frozen that way for a minute as it sinks in. And then we both burst out laughing.

25

Ben and Haley's Six-Year Anniversary

Ben

"You two call me if you need anything," Nina says as I walk her to the door. "Anything at all."

"Thank you, and you know we will." I kiss her on the cheek just before she exits onto the front porch.

It's no secret how many times we've called her at all hours of the day and night since Jackson arrived. And now she's helped us get settled after another happy surprise. We just came home from the hospital a few hours ago with our brand new baby girl. We went back and forth with a lot of names, especially since our first kid came with one assigned to him already, and we kept our discussions private, not wanting outside interference. Late last night, we settled on Jillian Nanette, the middle name, of course, being for Aunt Nan.

Life can be funny. One day you have no babies at all, and less than a year later you suddenly have two! Haley did her usual freak out over that throughout the pregnancy, but she's a great mommy to Jackson, and she'll be a great mommy to our new little bundle of joy, too. And even though fate didn't make this the little boy Grandpa Ed wanted in his lineage, I'm pretty sure he's still smiling down on us all.

Haley is tired, but feeling fine otherwise. And though Nina and Paul offered to keep Jackson for our first night at home with our perfect little newborn, we decided we were up to the challenge of handling them both, come what may. "Might as well get used to it," Haley said. And we both know we may be in for quite a ride for the foreseeable future, but we couldn't be happier about it.

As Nina drives away, I run my hand back through my hair, tired myself—but fulfilled. I stand quietly in the foyer of the beautiful home I share with my amazing wife and now my kids, the skyline visible out the tall back windows in the distance. Not bad for a poor kid orphaned at ten.

Back when I was feeding dogs at Grandpa Ed's kennel—hell, even when I was busy earning my degree at UC—I couldn't have dreamed life would turn out so great. And just now, the realization makes me think of Aunt Nan's wedding gift. Because even if we'd *never* opened it, all the good things in my life came from the same core message that box contained: It was about giving love away. I was afraid of that once—and now it's all around me.

Letting out a happy sigh, I step back inside to find Haley on the couch, her head leaned back, looking like I feel: exhausted but good. "How's everything in here?" I ask.

"Both babies are asleep!" she whispers excitedly.

"Nice," I say with a small fist pump. Jackson is in his

room—newly moved in order to vacate the nursery for the new arrival, and our daughter is in a crib across the room.

Haley glances toward the kitchen counter, where a small cake rests. Today is our anniversary, so Hannah surprised us with it from the bakery—we came home to find it waiting there. "Wanna eat cake?" Haley suggests.

"Tempting idea," I say, "but you probably need something better than cake for dinner."

"There *is* nothing better than cake for dinner."

We share a silent laugh, and I suggest, "Why don't we dip into the wedding box? We probably have a pizza or two left in there and we can have it delivered, with cake for dessert."

"Fair enough," she says. "I'll go look."

While she's gone, I finally have a minute to text Terrence. I already let him know we had a healthy baby girl, but this I the first chance I've had a send a picture. I attach the photo, then type: *Meet Jillian Nanette Page, all 7.5 pounds and 19.7 inches of her!* I proudly hit Send.

A minute later he answers and I pick up my phone expecting accolades and compliments, but to my surprise I see: *Are you kidding me, bro? Jack and Jill. I was only kidding about that at the wedding, you know?*

Oh. Oh my God.

What have we done?

"Haley!" I call. I don't even care if I wake the babies. "Haley, we have a problem!"

She comes rushing back into the room, looking harried and worried, Aunt Nan's gift box in her hands. "What? What's wrong?"

"We've named our children Jack and Jill."

Haley

"Okay, that's awful," I say. Because seriously, how did that not cross our minds?

Well, I *know* how. Jillian wasn't even in the running until yesterday when I met a nurse with the name and liked it. I guess exhaustion took over and kept me from putting two and two together. I'm not sure what *Ben's* excuse is—but I keep my cool. Becoming a mommy has taught me how to be less reactive and more steady, at least in *some* ways. So I calmly announce, "No, we've named them Jackson and Jillian, and we'll never call them anything but. Ever."

Hopefully that works and we don't become the laughing-stocks of the PTA. And I love both names. Plus they're in keeping with our same-letter family tradition, which I think I slid right past Ben.

"Jackson and Jillian," he says, clearly trying it on for size. Then he laughs good-naturedly. "Is it crazy that I actually like it?"

Smiling, I take his hand and lead him to the cake with *Happy Anniversary, Ben and Haley* written on top. Grabbing a knife, I carve two little slices. "We can order pizza in a few minutes, but for now, happy anniversary, Mr. Page." I pick up one little sliver of cake and hold it up to his mouth, feeding it to him, just like on our wedding day.

He follows suit with, "Happy anniversary, Mrs. Page," feeding me a bite of cake, as well.

Then we share a sweet, sugary kiss.

It's getting dark out, and all the inside lights are off, so we're standing in the shadows, eating cake and kissing.

Distant city lights provide the perfect backdrop for a moment that makes me remember every road we've traveled to get here. The rocky ones, the smooth ones, and tiny, narrow Blissful Lane have all led to this perfect pinpoint in time.

But then practicality takes back over—Ben looks for a pizza gift card and I shift my attention to our new daughter, swaddled in a pale pink blanket.

"My only regret," I say softly to Ben, "is that Aunt Nan isn't here to meet our baby girl." I mean, in my heart, I know she is. I know because of the purple cats on Jackson's baby blanket. But life has gotten busy since that fated day—adoption prep, becoming a mommy, experiencing my first pregnancy, and all while running a bakery. It's been a lot, and maybe I haven't focused as much since then on whether I still feel her with us.

When the doorbell rings, we both flinch. "Who could that be?" Ben asks.

"Maybe Mom forgot something," I say. I don't think anyone else would show up tonight without calling first. Just like when Jackson came home, we're having a baby meet-and-greet this weekend.

Together, we head to the door and Ben pulls it open.

No one's there.

But we spot a white, unmarked delivery van leaving in the distance, already on its way back up Blissful Lane. "That's weird," he says.

It's then that our eyes drop to the porch where we see a large gift basket containing:

A bouquet of daisies.

A box of donuts—and at a glance, I'm pretty sure they're jelly.

And a stuffed purple cat.

Tied to the basket's handle are a bunch of purple balloons.

Ben and I just look at each other, mouths gaping. He shakes his head. "I don't know what to say."

But I just laugh and tell him, "I do." Then I step out onto the porch and into the front yard, where I look up through the trees to the stars just beginning to twinkle in the night sky and say, "Aunt Nan, you give the world's best gifts!"

Also by Toni Blake

The Summer Island trilogy

The One Who Stays

The Giving Heart

The Love We Keep

The Rose Brothers trilogy

Brushstrokes

Mistletoe

Heartstrings

The Coral Cove trilogy

All I Want is You

Love Me if You Dare

Take Me All the Way

The Destiny Series

One Reckless Summer

Sugar Creek

Whisper Falls

Holly Lane

Willow Springs

Half Moon Hill

Christmas in Destiny

Return to Destiny

Standalone Novels

Wildest Dreams

The Red Diary

Letters to a Secret Lover

Tempt Me Tonight

Swept Away

The Mandy Project

The Perfect Mistake

The Weekend Wife

The Bewitching Hour

The Guy Next Door

The Cinderella Scheme

About the Author

Toni Blake's love of writing began when she won an essay contest in the fifth grade. Soon after, she penned her first novel, nineteen notebook pages long. Since then, Toni has become a RITA™-nominated author of more than twenty-five contemporary romance novels, her books have received the National Readers' Choice Award and Bookseller's Best Award, and her work has been excerpted in *Cosmo*. Toni lives in the Midwest and enjoys traveling, crafts, and spending time outdoors.

www.toniblake.com

Printed in the USA
CPSIA information can be obtained
at www.ICGtesting.com
LVHW090200090424
776840LV00004B/53